Anywhere Else but Here

Thirteen-year old Molly Smelter wants to get out of Schenectady, New York, and make a fresh start somewhere else. She and her widower father are close, and living with her aunt isn't too bad, but her aunt's "fiancé," Mr. Shelby Bissel, sets Molly's teeth on edge. Especially since she suspects he was the real cause of her father's printing business going bankrupt. Into an already trying situation comes Fostra Lee Post, a platitude-quoting member of a self-actualization group, whose eight-year-old son, Claude, is one of the least likable children Molly has ever met. Fostra Lee seems to have more than passing interest in the Smelter family. Obviously, it's time for desperate measures to be taken.

Molly's determination to save her decent (if not daring) father from the machinations of both Shelby Bissel and Fostra Lee triumphs over setbacks that would flatten a less strong-minded heroine. "In the end Molly's victory is all the sweeter because she's pursued her dream both with gumption and a good heart."
—*School Library Journal*, starred review

BY BRUCE CLEMENTS

Two Against the Tide

The Face of Abraham Candle

From Ice Set Free

I Tell a Lie Every So Often

*Coming Home to a Place
You've Never Been Before*
WITH HANNA CLEMENTS

Prison Window, Jerusalem Blue

Anywhere Else but Here

ANYWHERE ELSE BUT HERE

by Bruce Clements

FARRAR · STRAUS · GIROUX

New York

Copyright © 1980 by Bruce Clements
All rights reserved
First printing, 1980
Printed in the United States of America
Published simultaneously in Canada by
McGraw-Hill Ryerson Ltd., Toronto
Designed by Gwen Townsend

Library of Congress Cataloging in Publication Data
Clements, Bruce.
Anywhere else but here.
[1. Single-parent family—Fiction] I. Title.
PZ7.C5912An   [Fic]   80-11345
ISBN 0-374-30371-1

For Lisa, who brightens all of Minnesota
and large sections of nearby states

Anywhere Else
but Here

Chapter 1

Papa and I had an auction last July 8 and sold everything in the house except what belonged to my aunt. We had a lot of debts on our printing business, which had gone broke during the winter, and we wanted to pay our bills and get out of Schenectady, New York, and start fresh someplace else. (At least, that's what I wanted. Papa wasn't so sure about going away.) All day Friday, July 7, the only thing on my mind was getting everything ready so that we could make as much money as possible. That sounds greedy, I guess, but I don't mind.

Dragging everything out of the house and selling it didn't bother me, or at least it didn't bother me very much. Sometimes you just have to start your life all over again. My mother did that when she was only eleven. She had to flee the Russians when they came into Poland in 1944, and leave everything behind except one suitcase.

She and my father made a great couple. For a long time after they were married they thought she would never get pregnant, but they kept trying, and after fifteen years I was there. I don't think I'll ever get married, but if I do I'd want it to be romantic, like their marriage was. They never stopped loving each other or wanting to be together. She died of cancer when I was eleven months old.

So there it was, Friday, July 7, and I was getting things ready for the auction. It was a hot day, but there was a little breeze and the humidity wasn't bad. I had put sheets on the line in the back yard around ten, and by eleven they were dry. (Sheets smell great when you dry them outside, and it doesn't cost electricity.) We were living in a big white house on Palmer Avenue with a porch that ran all the way across the front and down the side. In front of the porch, like a screen, there were tall lilac bushes, so you could sit on the porch and watch people go by and not be seen if you wanted to.

I was in the downstairs hall gluing labels on cardboard boxes, some of them full of junk but most of them with really good things in them, when the doorbell rang. I didn't exactly look beautiful. I was sweaty, and I had plaster in my hair (I didn't know about the plaster until a few minutes later when Aunt Aurora told me to go brush it out), and my glasses were halfway down my nose, which they always are, and I had a cut on the back of my hand that I was sucking. I thought it was probably Phillip Reinauer collecting for the newspaper, but it was a man in an expensive suit. I pulled my hand out of my mouth and pushed my glasses up my nose and asked him if I could help him. He didn't seem to notice how terrible I looked, or maybe he didn't care. "Miss Smelter," he said, "I'm Walter Potrezeski. I saw your advertisement concerning the auction in the *Polish-American Club News*. Is your father at home?"

I recognized him, but I didn't know his name. I had seen him lots. Every time there was some special event at the Polish-American Club, he would come and stare at me. Mary Ellen Cox, my best friend, noticed him first and pointed him out to me. Whenever my group was dancing, he practically didn't look at anybody else. (Mary Ellen had moved out of Schenectady in April, which was another reason I didn't want to stay.)

I told him that Papa wasn't home. He didn't move, he just put out his hand, and we shook hands. "I came to Schenectady today on business," he said, "and I thought I might be able to see some of the things you will be offering at the auction sale tomorrow. Am I correct? It is tomorrow?"

"Oh, yes, but we still haven't got everything ready. We'll have it all out on the side porch and in the yard tomorrow morning. Maybe you could come early and take a look at it."

He smiled as if he knew something I didn't, which always makes me feel funny.

"Well, excellent," he said. "Do you by any chance have a list of the items you will be selling?"

I shook my head. "No, I'm sorry, I don't." (That was a lie. I did have a list, but I had only one copy of it, and I didn't want to let it go. All I wanted was for him to leave.)

"According to your advertisement, you have Danzig china."

"Yes, from my mother's aunt in Canada. We have a complete set of dishes for twelve, with nothing even chipped. I hope you'll be able to come back tomorrow."

"Oh yes," he said. Still, he didn't move. "You look a great deal like your mother when she was young. Did your Canadian aunt ever tell you that?"

"She died before I was born."

"Well, you do. You should wear your *sukmana* tomorrow."

"It isn't ironed," I said, as if that was the only reason I wouldn't wear it. "It would be awfully hot in weather like this, anyway. Well, if you'll excuse me, I have some boxes I have to finish in here."

He smiled again, and we said goodbye, and he turned

5

around and walked down the porch stairs. I felt a little creepy. How did he know what Mama had looked like when she was young? I shut the door and went and glued the last few labels on the boxes, and then I went through the kitchen and out into the back yard to see Aunt Aurora, who was sitting next to the garage in a beach chair reading the biography of an old movie star. She shut her book with her finger in her place and looked up at me, squinting because the sky was so bright.

"A crocodile was just here to see you," I said. "Or maybe it was a large lizard. Sometimes it's hard to tell the difference. Anyway, I told him you were busy, so he went away. He had big teeth, and a long green tail, and he was smoking a cigar. That's why I didn't let him in."

She just kept looking up at me and smiling and squinting, so I sat down on the grass and waited for her to say something. Aunt Aurora is a pretty woman. She had just finished a diet, so she really looked great. When I was little, she was the biggest part of my life. She was around while Papa was at the printing shop, and took care of me. But by the time I was thirteen, even though I still liked her, I didn't have too much respect for her, mostly because she was engaged to Mr. Shelby Bissel, who used to be Papa's business partner. For six years he had been telling her that they were going to get married as soon as his rich uncle in England died, and all that time Aunt Aurora believed it, or at least she acted as if she did. In fact, Uncle Shel could sound so sincere that sometimes even *I* believed it. It's terrible to see somebody lied to, even if they want to be, and Aunt Aurora didn't deserve it, because she was really a very nice person.

After I had been sitting in front of her for a while chewing on a piece of grass, she asked me who had really come to the door.

6

"It was somebody asking about the auction," I said. "I told him to come back tomorrow."

"That's nice. Remember that I want you around here the day after. Some of the neighbors are loaning us furniture to fill in, and I want you to help carry and put things where they belong. So remember, don't come up with something else on Sunday."

"I'll remember."

"I don't want to be after you. You have plaster or something in your hair. Go get a brush and brush it out, and while you're inside, go to the refrigerator and get me a glass of lemonade with two ice cubes in it. It's in my prune-juice jar."

I stood up but I didn't move. "Aunt Aurora, can I ask you a question?"

"If it's about moving away from here, I don't want to talk about it. You and your father can leave Schenectady if you want to. I can take care of myself. I have money coming in every month, and I'm not alone in the world."

"It isn't about that," I said. "It's about something else. Did Mama know a man named Potrezeski, do you know? That was the name of the man at the door, and he said I looked like Mama when she was young."

"Your mother was a very warm, friendly woman. She had a lot of friends. Has the mailman come yet?"

"I don't think so. Do you want me to look?"

"No, you don't have to bother, but you can get my lemonade. And you may have a glass, too, if you want one."

She opened up her book and started reading again, so I went and got her her lemonade, and then I went for a run down Palmer Avenue, across Union Street, and into the park and back. Usually when I'm running I don't think about anything at all, which is probably one reason I like to do it, but this time I started thinking about Aunt Aurora. I could see myself trying to get out the front door carrying my suitcase, and her standing in front of me and not letting me. To get that picture out of my mind, I began to run very fast and try to add up in my head all the money we might get for different pieces of furniture. I knew we'd never get what anything was worth. For instance, there was a floor lamp with a double head in my bedroom. I probably read two hundred books under that lamp, which was just the right height for my bed, but nobody would care about that. (It was the first thing we sold the next day, and we got $4.25 for it.)

I tried not to be mad at Aunt Aurora, because I felt sorry for her. She had had a hard life, even though it might not sound that way. Right after secretarial school she had gone to work for two brothers who were in the real-estate business. They were almost sixty and they were bachelors, but they both fell in love with her anyway. They couldn't both marry her, so they decided that neither of them would. (She wouldn't have said yes anyway, because it would just have been for the money, and she isn't that kind of person.) For ten years they bought her a new car every birthday to come to work in, and at Christmas they gave her a lot of expensive perfume and jewelry. (She still has all the jewelry and about a hundred bottles of perfume.) The two brothers died very close to each other, and when the second one went she got a trust fund paying her $200 a month for life, which was a curse for her. She moved in with us and never got a job again.

When I came back from running, Uncle Shel was sitting on the front porch sipping a glass of wine and reading the newspaper. Before I went inside, the two of us had a deep conversation.

"Hello, Uncle Shel."

"Hello there, Molly, how are you?"

"Fine. How are you?"

"In the pink. Been working hard getting ready for tomorrow?"

"I guess so."

"Don't complain. Someday you'll look back and realize that these are the best years of your life."

"I wasn't complaining. Well, I'm going inside and take a shower."

"Have a good time. You got some white stuff in your hair. Been baking a wedding cake for your aunt and me? You might have to be doing that sometime very soon, you know.. Would you like that?"

I went into the house without answering. While I was washing my hair I made a list of all the good things I could think of about him. It wasn't too long a list, and I remember it exactly.

1. Shelby Bissel has clean toenails.
2. Shelby Bissel never picks his nose while playing cards. (This is very important. Mary Ellen had a cousin who used to do that all the time, even when he was dealing.)
3. Even though she isn't his mother, Shelby Bissel always brings Aunt Aurora a candy heart on Mother's Day.
4. Shelby Bissel always folds the newspaper back up when he is finished with it.

That's it.

The fact is, he was really close to being a crook. The winter before, when he already knew that the business was in terrible shape, he had begged Papa to buy out his half. I was at the shop cutting paper at the time, which is how I know that "begged" is the right word. After they talked for a while Papa said yes, without looking at the books or seeing what a mess the billing was in, even though he had to take out a personal loan from the bank to do it. I'm not sorry, because the business would have gone broke anyway and this hurried it up, but it was a sneaky thing for Uncle Shel to do. After that, I thought he was about the worst person in the world, male or female. (That was before I met Fostra Lee Post, who seemed wonderful at first but turned out to be worse.)

By the way, it's hard work to go broke. You send out third-notice bills that cost you stamps but never get paid, and you get copies of bills you thought were paid long ago, and people mail you checks or come in and pay bills because they've heard you're in trouble, but by then it's too late for the money to help, but still you're glad, and you have to fill out all kinds of forms for the bank and the government. Mostly, you find out how terrible your filing system is, because you can't find what you're looking for.

After my hair was dry, instead of going back downstairs I stayed upstairs and played with my dollhouse, which I wasn't going to sell no matter what. Some people might think it's a little strange to be playing with a dollhouse when you're not a little girl any more, but I don't feel that way. I like all kinds of toys. I even like water pistols. Mary Ellen and I used to have water-pistol fights every summer until she moved away. Even now, whenever I see a water pistol in a store I always want to find out how far it will shoot and how accurate it is and how many squirts you can get out of it before you have to refill it. Maybe that doesn't seem grownup, but I don't mind.

Chapter 2

The dollhouse I stayed upstairs playing with was my mother's. It was an exact model of her house in Krakow, complete with a tiny brass plate on the side door with a number on it. The house had two floors and an attic, plus a tiny garden in the back with grass and three rosebushes. On the first floor there was a big music room, an even bigger living room, a dining room, and a kitchen. The dining-room table had a glass bowl of fruit on it, and six chairs, and the music room had a grand piano with a stool that you could turn up and down. There was a marble fireplace in the living room, and hanging over it was a painting of my mother as a little girl, with her head turned a little bit, as if she was just starting to look over her left shoulder.

There were no dolls in the house, which would have spoiled it, but there was a dog sleeping in front of the fireplace and a canary in a cage next to the window in the master bedroom. (There was a balcony on the second floor, too, and sometimes I would move the canary out there.) The house was put together with wooden pegs, and there was a special suitcase that went with it that all the furniture and the walls fit into. It was the only thing Mama took with her when she ran away from Krakow.

Whenever I took the house apart I would think about Mama doing it the day the Russians were coming, and I would start listening for the guns and feeling a little afraid myself. Sometimes I would purposely pack the house and unpack it and pack it up again just to get that feeling. Of course I knew there was no real danger, but I think I got a little closer to her by doing it.

In a way, the dollhouse was a second home to me, a place where I could go and be by myself whenever I wanted to. I did all sorts of things there. I had afternoon tea in the garden, I cooked in the kitchen on the cook's day off, I sat next to the fireplace petting the dog, and I had dancing parties that went on all night. (When the parties were over and my fiancé and I were the only ones left, except for the orchestra, we would dance out into the garden and watch the sunrise.) Everybody in the house sang all the time, especially the maids, except when I was sick in bed, and then they would be very sad and worried and walk around on tiptoe, but after I got well again they would sing louder than before.

Also, the cook made great Polish ice cream.

What I really wanted to do after Papa and I got all our debts paid was to go to Willimantic, Connecticut, where Papa had heard about a small printing business being for sale, and find a house exactly like Mama's (except for the maids), and move into it and live happily ever after. That was really just a dream, I know, but sometimes you get an idea in your mind and you think that that's the most important thing in the world and you've got to make it come true. In fact, I had never been to Willimantic or even seen a picture of it, but that didn't make any difference to me.

When I was through playing with the house I wrote a letter to Mary Ellen Cox in Philadelphia.

Dear Mary Ellen,
How is everything? How are your parents? How is Maureen? The stick of gum in this letter is for her. I met

your grandmother downtown yesterday (well, actually it was Tuesday) and she showed me pictures of your new house. It looks *great!*

Tomorrow is the auction, so tomorrow night everything in the house, not counting Aunt Aurora's furniture, will be gone. I am keeping some cardboard boxes of clothes and books and some suitcases with winter things in them, and of course the dollhouse. I would never sell that.

Pretty soon we'll be out of Schenectady, I hope. Remember that man you used to say watched me whenever I was dancing? Well, he came to the door today asking about the auction. He told me I looked like my mother when she was young. How would he know that? After he was gone I told Aunt Aurora that a crocodile had come to see her. She didn't think that was funny. I think she was right. Why do I say things like that?

Did you hear that Bobby Wilson's father bought an apple orchard, and Bobby buried his Uncle Ken's sword there? Isn't that weird?

Love,

Molly

P.S. I must inform someone somewhere! Out under Robert Wilson's apples lies Ken's sword.

Write back. That's an order.

Molly

The P.S. looks dumb, but that's because it's in a code Mary Ellen and I had. The first letter in each word spells out a message.

I must have been walking very quietly when I went downstairs, because when I came into the kitchen I caught Uncle Shel kissing Aunt Aurora in front of the oven. It was a real movie kiss, with Aunt Aurora bent back, and it shocked me because I had never seen them kiss that way before. I acted as if I hadn't seen it, but of course that was ridiculous. "I wanted to ask you if you wanted me to set the table," I said.

Aunt Aurora went over to the cup cabinet and picked up a letter that was hanging over the edge of a shelf. "I was just telling your Uncle Shel that we're having a visitor come and see us before long. Isn't that nice?"

I didn't answer.

"She's the oldest and best friend I have," Aunt Aurora said. "I don't mean she's old, but she's the one I've had the longest. Well, she's coming to see me."

She handed me the letter and then took it back right away. "When she wrote this she still wasn't sure about her plane times. She's going to call me when she gets to New York from California. Her name is Fostra Lee Post. I'm sure you've heard me talk about her."

"Not that I can remember," I said. "Shall I set the table now? It's getting time."

She opened the silverware drawer and the dish cabinet for me, and I went and started to set the table in the dining room while she and Uncle Shel whispered in the kitchen. I felt sorry for her. It's terrible to have to kiss and hug in front of somebody else's kitchen stove, especially if you're middle-aged. When I was finished with the table she came and inspected it and asked me about the cut on the back of my hand, which I had forgotten. "It's all right," I said. "I got it when I was getting some stuff out of the basement."

"Did you put antiseptic on it?"

"Not yet, but it stopped bleeding long ago, and it's clean."

She shook her head. "A thirteen-year-old girl shouldn't have to be up and down in the basement working all day," she said. "You used to play tennis with Mary Ellen Cox. You haven't done that this summer once yet."

"She's moved."

"I know that. It's all this turning the house upside down that makes me forget. Anyway, you need to get more exercise than you're getting."

"I went out running before."

Aunt Aurora waved her right hand in the air the way she always did when I said something she didn't like. "Running is for boys. You could play tennis with that poor Reinauer boy next door." (She always called him "that poor Reinauer boy," because his parents were divorced and he was living with his grandparents. Actually, they were nice people and he liked it.)

"Phillip thinks he's too big for tennis. It's stupid, but that's the way he thinks. Also, he's already practicing up for football. He's probably at Linton right now, running around the track or lifting weights or something."

Aunt Aurora waved her hand again and shook her head. "Well, I certainly wouldn't want you to play football. Why don't you just go out on the porch and sit down and rest and wait for Papa? Your Uncle Shel and I have some things to talk about. Everything seems to be happening at once. That's the way of the world, I guess. Go on, now."

I went. Sitting on the porch steps, I made up a multiple-choice question to fit Aunt Aurora.

MULTIPLE CHOICE QUESTION
If a sneaky, selfish man who eats at your house almost every day tells you that he's going to marry you as soon as his rich uncle in England dies, what should you do?

   a) Run out and buy a wedding cake.
   b) Order a wedding gown fitted to your precise measurements.
   c) Call a priest and tell him to get ready.
   d) All of the above.
   e) None of the above.   Answer: ____

Papa came home around six and I reminded him that we were going to go to the drive-in. "Right, I had forgotten," he said. "We both need to see a movie." (That's one of the things I like about my father. When he says yes to something you want, he never acts as if he's doing you a big favor, even when he is, though actually I think he *did* want to go to the movies.)

Halfway through dinner, the phone rang. It was Fostra Lee Post calling from New York. She and her eight-year-old son were about to get on a plane for Albany.

"We're waiting for you," Aunt Aurora said, stepping back and forth and wiggling around like a little girl. "We wouldn't let you stay anywhere else. It's an awful mess in the house, but don't worry about a thing. My fiancé and I will be waiting at the airport when you arrive, and we have lots of room. Stay as long as you like. The longer the better. We'll have beds next to each other, the same way we did at camp."

Aunt Aurora went on talking, asking her how the weather in California was and how her plane ride to New York had been and things like that, and then she said good-bye and just stood there with the phone in her hand looking at me. "Fostra Lee Post is the best friend I ever had," she said. "You'll love her, Molly. Imagine that! The last time I saw her was over twenty years ago. Would you believe that? We went to church camp together. We were close friends from the first minute we saw each other."

Uncle Shel put more food on his plate and started to eat faster. "This is just the thing you need," he said to me with his mouth full of mashed potatoes. "She'll bring a little life to the house, and you'll have someone around to play with. Ever since your friend went to Rochester, you've been lonely."

"Molly's friend went to Philadelphia," Papa said, "and I'm not sure that what she needs right now is an eight-year-old playmate."

"Well, it looks like she's going to get one," Uncle Shel said, looking at me and grinning. "And your girlfriend's name was Mary Lou, right?"

"It's Mary Ellen."

"Well, I'm close. I got her first name, which is better than half right. Don't you think that's right, that the first name is more important to remember than the second?"

I didn't answer. It was really embarrassing the way he had to prove all the time that what he said was right.

Aunt Aurora went into the kitchen and brought the pie to the table and went upstairs to get dressed. A minute later she came bouncing down wearing earrings and smelling of perfume. "I'm ready," she said, and stood behind Uncle Shel's chair until he pushed it back and got up.

"It's too bad your friend is flying in before I get my new car," he said going out the front door. "I've always said that a good-looking woman deserves a Cadillac."

After they went down the porch stairs the house was suddenly very quiet. I thought about the drive-in movie, but I didn't say anything. The main feature didn't start until after ten, and I thought maybe Mrs. Post and her son would be tired before then and Papa and I could still go. We went in the kitchen and did the dishes, and Papa told me everything he knew about Fostra Lee Post, which wasn't much. "She was just Fostra Lee when your aunt met her," he said. "I don't know if she had brothers and sisters or not. She never came to the house, but Aunt Aurora has written her letters three or four times a year from the time they met until now. Mrs. Post sends a Christmas card every year and sometimes something else. I remember your aunt getting a wedding invitation from her and then getting a letter a little while later saying that she was divorced."

"And she's beautiful, according to Aunt Aurora," I said, and I began to wonder if she might try to get Papa to fall in love with her and marry her. If she did, we'd stay in Schenectady, probably, and I'd get a stepmother and an eight-year-old stepbrother and otherwise no change in my life at all. It wasn't that I was against Papa falling in love. I just didn't want him to do it in Schenectady. After we got to Willimantic he could fall in love with anybody he wanted to and get married and even have children.

I decided I didn't want to talk about her any more. "Do you know a man named Potrezeski? He comes to the club whenever we have a big program and stares at me. He was here today."

"I remember you telling me that somebody was doing that. What did he come to the house for?"

"He wanted to look at what we were selling from Poland. I think he would have bought everything if I had let him in. There was a big lump in his jacket pocket exactly the size of a checkbook. He told me I remind him of Mama. That's why I thought you probably knew him. He said I looked like her when she was young."

"Did he say anything else?"

"Not about that. It was mostly just stuff about the auction."

"I stare at you a lot, too. I can't help it. You're a very good-looking girl."

"The only thing I want is not to be really ugly. I don't have to be beautiful. I'm not really ugly, am I?"

"I don't answer dumb questions."

The phone rang. It was Phillip Reinauer from next door saying he wanted to come over. I thought Phillip was in love with me. At least, he had been acting that way for the last year, coming over, hanging around, walking to the store with me, buying me perfume at Christmas, and that sort of thing. He told me once that when he was twenty-three we'd be just the right ages for each other. (Why does the man always have to be older? Women live longer. It would be better the other way around.) He pretended it was a joke, but I think he really meant it at the time. Phillip always figured out everything ahead. He had planned his whole life out. He was going to go to college, and then to Harvard Business School, and then to work for a big insurance company and become a vice-president. He even knew the kind of house he was going to live in. He had drawn up plans for it. It looked exactly like his grandparents' house except that it had three bathrooms and a swimming pool and it was in a rich neighborhood.

"I want to show you something and find out what you think of it," he said. "I just finished it."

"I don't think I could look at it right now. We have guests coming any minute."

"Well, it's important. When are they going?"

"They're not. I mean, not for a while."

"What about after they go to bed?"

"Papa and I may be going to the drive-in then."

"I could come over just before you go."

"I think they're coming up the driveway. Can you see the car? I really have to go."

"I'll come up on your porch after it gets dark and wait. If I have to, I'll come to the movie with you. I can show it to you in the snack bar. It's really important."

"O.K."

I hung up and pushed my glasses up my nose and went to the front door and looked through the screen. Fostra Lee

Post was coming up the walk with Aunt Aurora, smiling at the house. She was wearing a white dress with gold trim, and she was even more beautiful than Aunt Aurora had said. I opened the door and they came into the hall. Aunt Aurora looked around and waved her hand at the cardboard boxes as if that would make them disappear. "You should have put all of these elsewhere, Molly," she said.

Mrs. Post put her hand on my arm. "I think they look fine," she said. "They show that somebody has been working very hard."

Uncle Shel came banging in with three suitcases and put them down next to the front closet, letting the screen door slam, and we all went into the living room. Mrs. Post walked right next to me. "Your aunt tells me you're a wonderful, hard-working person. May I kiss you?" Without waiting for an answer, she stopped me in front of the sofa and put her hands on my face and kissed me on the cheek, but very close to my mouth. Then she flopped down as if she had lived in the house all her life. "Ah, it's wonderful to be in a home," she said. "This is the most comfortable sofa I ever sat on. I'm never going to get up, unless Molly asks me to do something for her."

"Except for Molly's bed, that's the best piece of furniture we have," Aunt Aurora said, "and my brother's going to sell both of them tomorrow morning. Talk him out of it, Fostra."

Mrs. Post looked at Papa for what felt like a long time. "I wouldn't try to talk that man out of anything," she said. "Besides, auction sales are fun. I love to go to them. I may bid on this sofa myself." She leaned back and started to tell us about how she had gone up and down the California coast one time looking for just the right Spanish cupboard. She had long, naturally blond hair tied back with a black velvet ribbon, and beautiful brown eyes, and a soft, loving voice. I could imagine her as the Virgin Mary in a religious painting, sitting in candlelight nursing the baby Jesus and looking down at him with a holy expression on her face. If someone had come in then and told me that she didn't care about anyone else in the world but herself, I wouldn't have believed it.

Chapter 3

For a long time after she arrived, Mrs. Post didn't pay any attention to anybody but me. She asked me how I liked school and what I thought about Schenectady and who my friends were and whether I was a Republican or a Democrat and how I felt about wearing secondhand clothes. Only two other people in the world had ever acted really interested in my ideas and my values before. One was Papa, and the other was my fourth-grade teacher, Miss Simmons. (I still remember the day she asked me whether I thought George Washington was right or not when he refused to run for a third term as President. I don't know what I said, but it was great being asked.)

While Papa was passing around the iced tea, Mrs. Post took off her sandals and held her legs out in front of me. "Your aunt says you run. Do you think I have the feet and legs for running? Whenever I come to a new city I always register for a modern-dance course. Maybe at the same time I should find someone to run with. What do you think? Maybe I should buy jogging shoes, too."

"I don't really know anything about running," I said. "I just do it in tennis shoes."

She put her hand on my arm. "We could run to the park every morning and play tennis when we got there. How does that sound? Like fun?"

"Sure."

While she was talking, Aunt Aurora sat in the big chair next to the front window like a proud mother watching her child. Aunt Aurora looked about forty-five and Mrs. Post looked about thirty-one or thirty-two.

When Mrs. Post started talking about health clubs in California I remembered her son, so I asked her where he was.

"He's here," she said, looking around the room as if he might be hiding behind a chair or something. Then she looked back at me and shrugged her shoulders. "Claude's probably still out in the car, unless he's taking a walk or doing something else. He loves cars. He'd sleep in a car every night if you let him. Put him in a car and he's as happy as a clam."

"Should I go out and get him? He might not know what house to come to. It's pretty dark, now."

She smiled her beautiful smile. "Do what your inner person tells you to do," she said. "It will never lead you wrong."

I got up and went outside, but then I didn't go to the car right away. I stood on the porch for a minute and just looked around. The stars were out, so it was going to be good weather for the auction. That was great. Mr. Burkett, the auctioneer, had told me good weather could mean more. Across the street in the Bauers' house all the lights were on and there was the noise of a lot of people talking. It was always that way on Friday nights because the Bauers were a big family and everybody always came home weekends.

I went to Uncle Shel's car and opened the front door, which made the inside light go on. There was a boy squinting in the back seat, so I jumped inside and shut the door behind me fast.

"Hi," I said.

There was no answer.

"I'm Molly."

Still no answer.

"You're Claude. Your mother told me. We're glad you could come and visit."

I rolled down the front windows. It was a warm night, but the air outside the car was like winter compared to the air inside. It also smelled better. My eyes were used to the dark now, so I could see him pretty well. He had a wide, flat face, as if he always slept face down on a board, and he looked mean, like someone who was just waiting to grow up so that he could get revenge on the whole world. He was rubbing his right wrist back and forth on his right pants leg very slowly, but otherwise he wasn't moving. There goes the movie, I said to myself. We'll spend the whole night just getting him out of here.

I usually like children, but I didn't like this one at all.

I sat there and looked at him and tried to figure out why he wasn't talking. Maybe he was afraid. But he didn't look afraid. In fact, I was the one who was afraid. I thought he might suddenly jump at me and bite me. (I know that sounds like a dumb idea, but I really thought he might do it.) I took my hands off the back of the front seat and tried talking again. "Would you like to come in the house and have some cookies and iced tea? Are you hot? It's really hot in here, even with the windows open, isn't it? I could bring you something out. Would you like that? Shall I bring you something to drink?"

For about ten seconds more I watched him while he rubbed his wrist on his pants, and then my wrists began to itch, so I slowly got out of the car and shut the door and went back to the house. As I was going up the steps I saw Phillip sitting on the porch railing. I told him I'd come out as soon as I could.

"You going to the movies?" he asked, but I didn't answer.

When I went back into the living room, Aunt Aurora was telling Mrs. Post what a wonderful man Papa was, how he had kept a whole block of downtown businesses from going broke by getting the merchants together and organizing fairs and putting out potted trees and bringing the customers back. She sounded like somebody in a commercial. Then she started telling Papa how wonderful Mrs. Post was, giving him a list of all the cities she had lived in, and telling him how she had been elected camper-counselor when they were at church camp together and how all the girls had envied her beautiful clothes.

When Aunt Aurora was finished, I told Mrs. Post that Claude was still in the car. "I went in the car and told him he could come in, but I think maybe he's afraid to," I said.

Mrs. Post smiled and pushed her long blond hair back from her ears with both hands at once, slowly. "Trust, Molly, trust. He's following his own best interests at this point in time. When he no longer gets satisfaction from being in the car, when he becomes aware that being there is no longer a growth experience for him, he will come into the house. I'm sure you understand in your heart what I am trying to tell you."

"It's just that he didn't seem too happy there," I said. "I asked him if he was going to come in, but he didn't answer."

Mrs. Post smiled. "Molly, there are three questions I never ask Claude. I never ask him what he's done in the past, I never ask him what he's doing now, and I never ask him what he's going to do in the future. And he *knows*, as young as he is, not to ask me those questions either. He can *offer me that information* if he wants to, but I never ask him and he never asks me."

"Oh," I said.

"He eats what he chooses to eat, he sleeps where he

chooses to sleep, and most of all he feels what he chooses to feel. I never try to tell him that one thing is good for him or another thing is bad for him. He finds out for himself by experience, and so he truly learns from life."

That sounded to me like what you say to yourself when you're too lazy to *do* something. "Does that mean he'll sleep in the car all night?" I said.

She shook her head and smiled, and at that moment the screen door opened and he came in the house.

I excused myself and walked around Claude and went out onto the porch. Phillip was still sitting on the rail, and I sat down next to him. "Hi," I said.

"Hi."

"How are you?"

"O.K. How are you?"

"Fine. You still working at the Farmers' Market?"

"Yeah, mornings. Right after I finish the papers." He handed me a sheet of paper with a poem typed on it. "I want to know if you think it's good. You want to read it?"

"Sure."

"O.K."

"It's a poem."

"I know."

I got up and went to the living-room end of the porch, where there was light coming through the window.

MY LOVE, ___?___

Is she beautiful? Yes, that I know!
As beautiful as a summer moon
Hanging o'er the ocean's flow
Floating on the night bird's tune.

Her hair is like the moonlit night,
Her glance like the early dew,
Her lips are like the berry bright,
When the summer day is new,

Her bosom like two drifts of snow
That heaven has softly laid,
With the help of the winds that blow
Within some tree's tall shade.

But is she true? I do not know!
She might be like the changing moon
Or the ocean in its ebb and flow
Or some singer with a changing tune.
Or the town clock with its changing bell
Which tells us, "Only time will tell."

I came back and sat down and handed it back to him. "It's very nice," I said.

"I got the model for it out of an old magazine in my grandparents' attic, but I changed it a lot. You like it?"

"Sure."

I thought he was going to tell me it was for me and that I should keep it, but he didn't. "That's all I wanted to know," he said, and got off the rail and went down the stairs and into the dark. I sat there for a minute wondering why he hadn't given it to me, and not even thinking that maybe he had found somebody else to be in love with, which proves that I can be pretty stupid if I want to be.

I went into the living room and told everybody I was going to go upstairs to bed. Claude was sitting in front of the fireplace rubbing the sharp end of the poker against the bricks. He had the same look on his face that he had had in the car. I never saw a child look so mean and so sick of everything. That was fine with me. The more miserable he was, the less he would want to stay.

When Papa came up to say good night, I asked him how long Mrs. Post was staying.

"She's going to a meeting at a motel in Albany next Thursday," he said, "and then she'll leave."

"Aunt Aurora wants you to marry her."

"Think it's a good idea?"

"I think, if you're going to marry anybody, it ought to be somebody who lives in Willimantic, Connecticut. What kind of meeting is she going to?"

"Mrs. Post belongs to a religion that has all of the answers to all of life's hardest questions. The headquarters is in Sacramento, California, and the god of this religion, whose name she told me but I forget, jumps into his jet plane every summer and brings wisdom to the east."

"Does she have a divorce?"

"Years ago."

"She's beautiful."

Papa nodded. "That's true."

Neither of us said anything for a minute, and then he started talking about Mama. "You walk like she did," he said. "Your legs must be hung the same way on your hips. She was the best, most complete friend I ever had. Did I ever tell you what a wonderful Polish accent she had when I first met her? The trouble is, she had such a good ear for languages that she had lost it by the time we were married and people couldn't tell where she was from, except that they knew it wasn't Schenectady. Now it's time for you to turn out your light."

He kissed me good night, but I kept holding his hand for an extra second. "Don't go to bed too late, Papa. The auction people are coming around seven to move things out."

"O.K."

He got up and left and I went and got the dollhouse out of the closet and brought it back to bed. There was bright moonlight coming in through the window, and the white bedspread made it look like a winter scene. I made believe it was four days before Christmas, and there was a party just beginning at the house. Mama, who was seventeen, was upstairs in the bedroom getting ready, putting on her earrings and taking a last look at her hair. Then she left her mirror and went to the window and stood watching the snow come down for a few minutes. A car with the last few guests came up the drive. "Oh dear, I'd better hurry," she said to herself in a whisper. The people got out of their car and walked to the door, their feet making a crunching sound in the snow, and before they finished ringing the doorbell Mama was already halfway down the stairs. The whole house smelled of pine boughs and spiced orange punch. She led the guests into the living room, which was cleared for dancing, and the piano and violins began to play, and everybody started whirling around. At the end of every dance Mama would turn around and there would be another partner waiting for her, until finally her favorite held on to her for dance after dance. It was a wonderful party, and it went on until Aunt Aurora and Mrs. Post came upstairs.

In real life, of course, by the time she was seventeen Mama had been out of Poland six years, and was in Canada waiting to come to the United States, and probably some Russian general or Communist Party official was living in her house. But in her imagination and in her dreams I'm sure she wore beautiful dresses and danced in that house all night just like I did.

Chapter 4

Saturday was sunny and not too hot, so it was a perfect day for an auction. There must have been two hundred people in our yard most of the time. Even the junk had bidders, and everything went very fast. Sometimes I thought Mr. Burkett was hurrying people too much and not giving them time to think, but I guess he knew what he was doing. My big bed, which was the only thing close to an antique in the house, sold for forty-two dollars, which was the highest price paid for anything.

I stood up on the side-porch rail most of the time, where I could look down on everything. Papa sat at a card table behind Mr. Burkett, making a list of how much was paid for each thing. Claude sat on the top porch step in his dark-blue wool suit rubbing his right wrist on his pants until it was bleeding, and Mr. Potrezeski sat in a folding chair in the front row and bought everything Polish that we had. (We got it all from Mama's aunt in Canada after she died. There wasn't much, but what there was was good.) Aunt Aurora and Mrs. Post stayed upstairs drinking coffee and talking. Every once in a while, even with all the other noise, I could hear Aunt Aurora giggling. It sounded nice.

After he had put all the china in his car, along with his chair, Mr. Potrezeski came up onto the porch to see me. I jumped down from the rail and tried to look friendly, and when he didn't say anything right away I told him I hoped he would like what he bought.

He nodded. "I'm certain I will."

"I hope so," I said.

"There is something I would like you to know," he said. "I knew your mother in Krakow when she was a young girl. We didn't meet formally until the night she and your grandmother left the city, but I had been observing her for a long time before that. That's why I was able to tell you how much you look like her."

I just stood in front of him not saying anything, so I guess he thought I didn't believe him.

"She lived at 42 Sokoljiew Street," he said.

"I think it was 46," I said.

He shook his head. "No, the side entrance was 46. The house was originally two apartments, 42 down and 46 up. When your grandparents bought it they made it into a single-family house and used the letter-box number, which was 42. That's why they had an oversized bathroom on the second floor. It was originally a kitchen. It was an excellent house."

I didn't say anything for a minute, wondering if I should tell him about the dollhouse. Finally I did, and asked him if he'd like to see it. He said he would, so I led the way upstairs.

When I went into my room, it was so empty I felt empty inside. There was nothing but a cot, folded against the wall, two cardboard boxes full of winter clothes, a box of books, and a suitcase. Even the posters on the walls looked different, as if they had suddenly gotten old.

I got the dollhouse out of the closet and put it on top of one of the cardboard boxes. Mr. Potrezeski looked at it for a long time. "It was an excellent house," he said again. "The grand piano was gone when I knew it. I don't know what happened to it."

"It's the only thing I'm not selling," I said.

He looked at me for a second as if he was sorry. "Did you know that your grandfather was a very religious man? That's why I'm alive. He knew he could be shot for sheltering Jews or Communists, and my father was both, but he believed that God wanted him to preserve life. He took us into the house when the first big roundup of Jews began. By then your grandparents were down to one servant, and they knew she'd keep us a secret because she was my mother's brother's widow. It was not a large house, as you can see, but it was grand. It was elegant, with large grounds in a first-class neighborhood. We lived there, in the attic, keeping very quiet most of the time. On Sunday mornings in summer I could look out of that window and see your mother and grandparents having breakfast together down in the garden. When there was no wind they would bring the canary bird out there to sing to them. It was such a peaceful scene. Very strange, such a thing in the middle of all that war. I was there until the Russians came. And all that time your grandfather sheltered us and fed us. It was hard on everyone. One night, I remember, after we had been in the house for about a year, he came up to see us. We had black curtains for the windows at night, and even then we never used a light except when one of us was sick. In any event, your grandfather came upstairs around midnight, carrying a candle, to talk to my father about some noises I had been making. My father apologized and said it would never happen again, and all of a sudden your grandfather's face got red and he put his two hands out right under my father's nose. 'Mr. Potrezeski,' he said, 'I took you into my house only for this, that God hates killing a tiny bit more than I hate Communism.' "

"What did your father say back?"

"Nothing. He was the guest, after all, and your grandfather was the host. I don't tell that story to take any credit from your grandfather. Just the reverse. He did good to us in spite of his desires, and that's the hardest kind of good to do. And I don't object to him hating Communism. I hate it myself. Fortunately for me, he was a believer in a good God."

"My mother never knew you were there?"

"Not until the hour before she left. I could tell that from the surprise on her face, even though she tried not to show it. Your grandfather had died the previous winter, which was very sad for us all. My father wept when that happened, and out of grief, not out of fear for himself. That last night, we stood in the kitchen with the guns booming in the distance and had a ceremony. My father made a short speech of thanks and your grandmother answered with a few words and gave him an envelope with the key to the front door in it. All the while your mother stood in a fur coat that was too big for her next to the door, very calm, as if she was waiting to go and see a play or hear a concert."

"Did they want to walk all the way to Germany?"

"Their plan was to keep going until they met the American Army. It sounds, now, like an insane thing to try to do, but it wasn't at the time. Your grandmother had some money and some jewelry sewn into her coat to buy help on the way. Certainly, it was an extremely dangerous thing to do, but staying was extremely dangerous, also. So they took their sandwiches and hard-boiled eggs and walked west. They were not alone."

"What happened to you?"

"After a few days the Russians came. When they found out that my father was a Communist they arrested him for being the wrong kind, and my mother for being the wife of the wrong kind. According to the Russians, all the true Polish Communists had spent the war in Moscow. I was too young to be dangerous, in their view, so they just put me in a labor brigade for a year and then let me go, and as soon as I was able I escaped to West Germany. After that I followed the same route your mother followed. I was three years behind her arriving in Canada, and five years behind her arriving in America. Not that I was intentionally following her. I spent ten years in this country finding my own way before I decided to trace her, and had the pleasure of watching you."

His saying that made me nervous. "I think I should go back out now," I said. "I have to see what's happening at the auction. My father may want me to do something."

We went downstairs and out onto the porch. Claude was still sitting there on the top step. He turned his head and looked at us, and Mr. Potrezeski and I both said hello, but he just sat there and stared, and Mr. Potrezeski and I walked around him and out to the sidewalk. When we got there, he asked me if I might after all want to sell the dollhouse. "It would get a good price," he said.

"That's the only thing I'm not selling."

"Might you be interested in renting it, then?"

"I don't think so, thank you very much."

"We could draw up a lease for a year or six months, with all the terms clearly set out. I would enjoy having it around for a while."

"I don't think so," I said again. I wanted to ask him how much rent he would pay, but I was afraid to.

He reached in his pocket. "Let me give you my card," he said. "I have an office in Saratoga. Here's the address and phone number. The address below is my home. Is the auction a sign that you intend to move away?"

"Yes. I'm not sure exactly when, but soon."

"Well, that's my loss," he said. "Thank you for showing me the house."

He went across the street and got in his car and drove away, and I went upstairs to put the dollhouse back in the closet, but before I got to my room, Aunt Aurora opened her door and waved to me.

"Mrs. Post and I want the news," she said. "Come in here."

"There's something I have to do," I said.   2097868

"It'll wait. This will just take a minute."

I went into her room and she shut the door. "Tell us what's happening at the auction."

"Nothing. People are buying things. Everything's selling. It's practically over."

Fostra Lee Post was sitting on Aunt Aurora's bed in a white satin dressing gown with white, fluffy feathers running down the front and around the collar. She got up and blew me a kiss and then went and looked at herself in the mirror on the closet door. Her dressing gown would have looked ugly on anybody else, but it looked fine on her. Really beautiful people, I guess, can wear anything, no matter what it looks like.

"There's just the last dribs and drabs to go," I said. "I thought it would take all day, but I guess it won't."

Aunt Aurora shook her head. "It can't be over too soon for me, I have work to do in the garden, if it isn't all trampled down."

"The garden's fine, Aunt Aurora," I said. "Papa tied a clothesline between the back porch and the ash tree so people would stay in the front yard. And the Reinauers' food table is all out of food. They sent Phillip to Gershon's Delicatessen twice to get extra stuff."

Aunt Aurora winked at Mrs. Post and then wagged a finger at me. "And I'll bet you went with him and maybe held hands when you got around the corner? It's nothing to be ashamed of."

"He's just a friend of mine who happens to live next door, Aunt Aurora. He's never been my boyfriend."

Mrs. Post walked across the room like a queen and sat down on Aunt Aurora's bed again. "Don't be in too much of a hurry to fall in love and get tied down to someone," she said. "You don't want to give up your freedom before you have it."

"He's just a friend," I said to her, but I was blushing.

"Good for you, Molly. We all need friends to celebrate life with us. I'm just about to get dressed and go for a walk, and I want you as my friend to come with me."

"I have to do something first," I said. "And I have to ask my father. He might need me."

Mrs. Post's dressing gown was already on the floor around her feet. She was naked. "He'll let you go," she said, starting to do stretching exercises, "After all, he wants you to be free, doesn't he? You must show me Gershon's Delicatessen where everybody buys all that wonderful food. Shall we take Claude along? Let's. Then you can get to know him better."

I went into my room and packed up the dollhouse. While I was doing it I thought about Snow White and the Seven Dwarfs. The real problem in Snow White is her father being stupid enough to marry the wicked queen in the first place, probably just because of her looks.

When I got downstairs Fostra Lee Post had already asked Papa if I could go with her, and he had said yes, so a minute later I was walking down Palmer Avenue with Mrs. Post on my right and Claude on my left.

36

When we got inside Gershon's, Claude asked me if I would get him a doughnut, so I went and asked Mrs. Post, who was busy looking at cheeses, if it was all right.

"Do you want to give him one?" she asked.

"I don't want to spoil his lunch."

She talked about cheese with the man behind the counter for a minute, and then looked at me. "Molly, don't make things hard for yourself when you don't have to. Claude is very clear about what he wants. Now, what do *you* want? Do *you* want to give it to him?"

"I don't have any money anyway."

She shook her head. "You're tuning out the true question, Molly. Money itself is never a problem, never, not as long as you know what you want. Do you want to give Claude a doughnut or not?"

"I guess I do."

She shook her head again. "Still a tune-out. Either you *don't* want to give him a doughnut, so you don't, or you *do* want to give him a doughnut, so you do. It's very simple once you see the question clearly."

"I do."

"Good. It happens that I want to pay for it, so I will. And we won't just get one, we'll get a dozen."

So we did.

Halfway back along Palmer Avenue, Mrs. Post stopped at the Sullivans' house and looked over the hedge. The Sullivans were away on vacation, so the grass in the front yard was a little long, but the flower beds in front of the porch were full of flowers. Mrs. Post looked at them. "Who lives here?" she asked.

"The Sullivans. Aunt Aurora knows them. Of course, she knows everybody."

Mrs. Post kept smiling. "They have a lot of flowers in the

back, too, I'll bet, and since they are obviously lovers of beauty, they'll be glad if we take some." She walked to the end of the hedge and up the driveway. I followed her, hoping that nobody was looking. Claude stayed out on the sidewalk. (Probably he had been on flower raids before.) There were all kinds of flowers back there, and Mrs. Post picked the best ones of each kind. "Buds that are just beginning to open are the best," she said when she handed me the second armful and went to pick some more. "When Mr. and Mrs. Sullivan come home, you must thank them so that they too can have pleasure out of this sharing," she said. "An empty house like yours deserves to have all the flowers it can get. Besides, it's fun helping other people to share, don't you think so?"

As we were coming back down the driveway she put her hand under my arm. "I wish I had someone like you to do things like this with all the time," she said. Claude was waiting for us, rubbing his wrist on his pants and eating a doughnut. (His third? His fourth? His fifth?) All the way home I was waiting for the police to pull up and arrest us.

"Maybe somebody should put a bandage on Claude's wrist," I said when we were back in our yard.

"Why?"

"It would keep him from rubbing it. I'm afraid he's going to get an infection."

She shook her head. "He won't get an infection unless he *wants* one, and if he wants an infection, we couldn't stop him from getting it no matter what we did. On the other hand, if Molly Cecilia Smelter wants to have the experience of putting a bandage on him, and if he wants to have the experience of having her do it, then the two of them can get together at any time and work it out."

"How did you know my middle name?"

"I asked your aunt. I'm very interested in you, Molly. You are a very very interesting person."

She went into the house and I went over to where Papa was working on the figures from the auction. We had made $534.67, which was about $65.33 less than the minimum we thought we would make. Well, there was nothing we could do about that.

Chapter 5

I talked to Papa for a little while, and then Mr. Burkett came over to give him a check and I went around to the back yard to see Aunt Aurora, who was digging weeds from around her new marigold plants. She stopped and picked up a newspaper and waved it at me. "There's something in the want ads that your father will want to know about. You can take it around and show it to him now."

In the middle of the page, with a red circle around it, was a big ad from General Electric. It had a list of all the kinds of people they were looking for, and Aunt Aurora had put a line under "Printers."

"I don't think he plans to stay in Schenectady, Aunt Aurora," I said.

I started to hand it back to her, but she wouldn't take it. "A good job at G.E. is a very good opportunity for someone with family responsibilities," she said.

I didn't want to get into an argument, but I didn't want to act as if I agreed with her, either. "I just think, now that the auction's over, he'll probably want to go to Connecticut and look at that printing shop in Willimantic before he thinks about doing anything else," I said.

She waved her hand in the air. "Go show that advertisement to him, and let him make up his own mind. You may do some grownup things, young lady, but you're not grown up yet. Your father has more important things on his mind than going off to Connecticut. G.E. is good to its employees. Go on, now, take it to him."

So I took it to him. (Adults make children do things like that all the time, as if it was good for you to do things against your own ideas.) I was sure that Papa didn't want to go to work for General Electric, and I think Aunt Aurora knew he didn't want to, too. That's why she asked me to bring him the ad. I was supposed to hand it to him and then stand there looking like a poor little girl who had to be taken care of. It was really more of an insult to him than to me. He knew what it meant to be a father. He didn't have to be told that he should take care of his child.

While he looked at the ad I watched two women and three men putting our living-room sofa into the back of a pickup truck that was really too short for it. Claude came down from the porch with the bag from Gershon's and handed it to me. There was one doughnut left. It was a little crushed, but I took it anyway.

"Did you eat the rest of them?"

"My mother had four."

The people drove away in the truck with three of them sitting on one end of the sofa to keep it from falling off, and Papa handed the paper back to me. "Did Boris give you this?"

"Yes."

"He knew the password?"

" 'The canary has escaped.' "

"And you gave him the proper answer?"

" 'The turkey is on its way.' "

"Why did Boris put a red circle around this particular want ad?"

"Maybe he wants you to read it."

"You might be right. Well, if you see him again, tell him I've already been to G.E."

"Why?"

"To see what kinds of jobs they had."

"Does that mean you're going to work there?"

"No, it just means I need to be working somewhere soon."

Fostra Lee Post came out on the porch. "After-the-auction tea is being served in the back yard," she said. "Your Aunt Aurora went upstairs to put on a dress, Molly, but you can come as you are."

We went around back. Mrs. Post had set up our old card table and put a beautiful white tablecloth on it. "It's a summer shawl of mine," she said. "If you're having after-noon tea, you *have* to have a tablecloth, that's all there is to it, and I couldn't find one of yours." There was a quart box of strawberries on the table, and a dish of sugar, and a jelly glass with some of the Sullivans' flowers in it, and birthday-party paper plates and napkins. I thought about Mama and her parents having breakfast in their back yard when she was a girl, and Mr. Potrezeski watching them from the attic. Mrs. Post passed out strawberries, giving me more than anybody. Claude didn't get any because he had never eaten strawberries. "I don't like strawberries. I never eat them," he said.

"We should have a canary bird out here to sing while we're eating," I said.

Mrs. Post smiled and shook her head. "You should never keep anything in a cage," she said. "It's against the laws of nature." She started talking about freedom, and the rest of us just listened, especially Aunt Aurora, who was wear-ing the pink summer dress she sometimes wore when she went to church. It was too big for her since her diet, so it looked as if she was wearing a bed sheet, but it was really very pretty. (She would have looked better in my Sunday dress, now that we were the same size.) After a while Mrs.

42

Post started feeding her strawberries with a spoon, like a baby, talking all the time, and Aunt Aurora smiled and ate. It was a nice thing for Mrs. Post to do, but it looked a little bit weird.

When the strawberries were gone she started talking about her plans. "I have a Short-Range Plan and a Long-Range Plan," she said. "Short Range, I'm going to attend the Growth Channel Assembly at the Thruway Motel in Albany, which is next Thursday. I have to get there early because I'm going to be on the Volunteer Staff. Not everyone gets on the Volunteer Staff. My Long-Range Plan is to keep on growing on the Good Energy Path."

"How will you know it's the right one?" Papa said.

Mrs. Post smiled. "You *always* know if you're traveling on the Good-Energy Path or not. All you have to do is consult your feelings. You've never heard one of Dr. Spiros Avanti's lectures, have you?"

Papa shook his head. "I've never even heard his name before."

"Really?" she said. Then she leaned over toward him and put her hand on his neck. "You'll hear his name more and more in the future. He's one of the great men of this century. He taught me how to stand alone in the world, and I love it. He gave me a new mind." She looked at me. "Be careful, Molly. Never give up your freedom. I say that to you because I think of you as my sister. That's the way I sincerely feel. We're at different life stages, of course, but I can see that you're moving on the Good-Energy Path, too. Every day I get freer and freer and more in tune with my true self. The only true sin on this earth is to keep another person from living freely. Did you know that? I would never do that. No one should ever do that. Will you remember that?"

I told her I would and excused myself and got up and

went inside the kitchen and closed the door behind me. Fostra Lee Post made me feel completely helpless, as if there was nothing I could do about *anything*. I looked in my pocket and found Mr. Potrezeski's card and went and dialed his office number. I didn't expect him to be there on Saturday afternoon, but he was. "Mr. Potrezeski," I said, "this is Molly Smelter. Could I talk to you sometime? I might want to rent the dollhouse, if you really meant it about renting it. Not permanently, of course."

"I'll take excellent care of it," he said. "It will be in very good hands."

"Well, I don't know if I want to rent it, but I'd like to talk about it." I turned around. Claude was standing in the door watching me. I turned my back to him and tried to speak softly, so he wouldn't hear. "I wouldn't do it, except I feel I should have some money of my own right now, and you were talking about the rent being in advance?"

"Absolutely. Would you care to have Sunday brunch with me at the Van Dyke Hotel? That's in Schenectady. Do you know it?"

"My aunt said today I should get out and do different things, so that'll be fine."

"Bring your aunt with you, if you wish. And of course your father is welcome."

"Thank you very much. I'll think about it."

"Shall we say at eleven o'clock tomorrow? Would it be convenient if I picked you up at your home?"

"No, thank you. I can meet you there."

The kitchen door opened and Mrs. Post came in with the empty strawberry box in one hand, almost knocking Claude down.

"Eleven o'clock is fine," I said, and hung up. I felt as if I had been caught doing something terrible, but Mrs. Post didn't even look at me. She grabbed Claude. "I love you so much I could eat you," she said, and turned him upside down and carried him outside. When she got in the middle of the yard she hugged him very hard while he hung there head down. "I'm never going to let you go," she said, and let him go.

Chapter 6

The rent money from the dollhouse was going to be my secret Get-out-of-Schenectady Emergency Fund, and I wasn't going to tell anybody about it, not even Papa. It's not that I wanted to keep it for myself. Money isn't one of the things I'm greedy about. In fact, the only thing I ever keep completely to myself is Halloween candy. I go out twice, once with the little kids and once with Mary Ellen, and keep it all in my drawer under my underwear. I usually forget it, and then every once in a while I discover it again and feel rich. (Have you ever eaten a nine-month-old popcorn ball?) So Saturday night I rolled around on my lumpy cot for a little while thinking about where I would hide the money and how I might spend it. For instance, I could buy a bus ticket and go to Willimantic and see the shop for myself. Or I could make long-distance calls to bankers.

When I was half asleep, I suddenly realized that I hadn't asked Mr. Potrezeski what rent he wanted to pay me. Maybe he thought I was just a little girl and he could pay me in lollipops or a necklace or something. I sat up. Maybe he'd try to put the rent in a bank account so I couldn't get at it until I was twenty-one. Well, the banks weren't open until Monday, and I would see him before he could do that, and make sure I got either cash or a check made out in my name.

I lay back down. Then I began to wonder how much rent I should charge, so I sat up again. Fifty dollars? Forty? Thirty? Thirty was too little. Forty sounded all right. I lay back down again. How did forty-five sound? How about forty-eight? Five dollars a month for twelve months? A dollar a week? That was less than five dollars a month, but it sounded like more. Well, that was probably too high, anyway.

When I fell asleep I was still thinking about numbers and I still hadn't made up my mind.

When I woke up it was after nine. It was a sunny morning, just perfect for sitting at a table in a nice hotel and eating like a pig. I got the dollhouse out of the closet and took it apart and put it in its suitcase. Problem: How was I going to get out of the house in my good dress, carrying a suitcase, without anybody knowing that I was doing something special? Answer: Just get dressed and go. Papa, I found out from a note on the bathroom mirror, was on a walk with Mrs. Post, and Claude was still asleep, and Aunt Aurora was downstairs whispering over breakfast with Uncle Shel, who had brought her a dozen long-stemmed roses in a glass vase that was in the front hall. (Those flowers were a clue to something, but I was too busy sneaking out with my suitcase to know it.)

"I'm going to church and staying downtown a little while, Aunt Aurora," I said as I got to the bottom of the stairs.

"Don't let the screen door slam," she said right after the screen door slammed.

It felt great. I was going on a combination date, secret mission, and business deal. In front of the house there was a big U-Haul truck that Uncle Shel had brought for collecting furniture from the neighbors. I felt a little guilty as I was walking by it, but on the other hand Aunt Aurora had told me I should get out more and have fun, and nobody else in the house was working yet.

I went to Mass at Saint John's, getting there halfway through the sermon, and at eleven o'clock I was sitting at a table across from Mr. Potrezeski in the garden behind the Van Dyke Hotel, looking at the menu and feeling the suitcase between my feet every two minutes to make sure it was still there. The waiter, dressed in a tuxedo, handed me the menu and stood behind me, but I couldn't make up my mind. "We'll order in a few minutes," Mr. Potrezeski said to him, "and while we're thinking we'll have a pot of tea and some orange juice."

The waiter said, "Of course," and went away. Mr. Potrezeski handed me an envelope. "Perhaps if we get our business completed first, we'll be free to enjoy our breakfast. It's the standard renter's lease. You'll notice that this space is empty. Do you have a rental figure in mind?"

"No, I don't."

"May I suggest one?"

"I thought about it last night, but I didn't come up with anything definite. All I decided was that it shouldn't be in lollipops." (I tried to smile as if that was a joke.)

"How would ten dollars a month suit you, with a half year's rent in advance, the other half due in six months?"

"I think that would be all right."

He took a pen from another pocket and wrote "$120.00" in the blank space. "There's a clause I should call your attention to on the second page. If you decide to sell the house, I have the right of first refusal, which means that you are obliged to offer it to me first. If I am not willing to pay your price, you're free to get that price anywhere, but you can't sell it for less without offering it to me again at the lower price."

"That sounds fair," I said, "but I'm sure I won't sell it." There were two copies, one for him and one for me, and I signed them both and he gave me a check for sixty dollars. "I think I'm ready to order now," I said, and I did, and in a few minutes I was stuffing myself. He had breakfast, too, but mostly he just watched me eat. I don't think he was really having breakfast with me. I think he was having breakfast with Mama. After a little while he began to talk about her.

"Your mother laughed a good deal," he said. "Sometimes we could hear her all the way up in the attic. She obeyed her parents. Children went to school in July in Krakow, and after she came home on clear summer days she would sit at the garden table, which was white like this one and about the same size, with a glass top, and do her homework. Sometimes her best friend would come over and they would work together or play. The friend's name was Casse, and she was very tall and thin. I think she must have been a year or perhaps even two years older. They were building a clubhouse behind the garage. It was a two-story affair, I mean the garage was, and it looked like an old-fashioned carriage house, except very narrow. She had your way of standing, or you have hers. She stood like someone on the platform at a train station peering over people's heads to see if the train was coming."

He stopped for a few seconds and smiled and took a sip of coffee. "I almost bumped into her once. It was in the middle of the night in the third year I was there, and I broke the cardinal rule and went down to the second floor and explored up and down the hall. All of a sudden there was a noise and a door opened, and your mother was walking across the hall to the bathroom. It was very dark, and she was half asleep, so she didn't see me, but I still feel ashamed of myself when I think of it. It was cruel to take a risk like that. I never came downstairs again, until the night your mother left. Did I tell you about the copper strip yesterday?"

"No."

"Well, your grandfather had a strip of copper nailed to the floor a half a meter back from the window, and we were never supposed to get closer to the window than that, day or night. I would stand with my toes just touching the edge and look out sometimes for hours, especially on nice summer days and whenever it was snowing. But you talk now. Please. I want to know about you."

I told him about the business and how I wanted to start high school in Willimantic in September. Once I got started, it was hard to stop, but after about fifteen minutes we got up and went through the hotel lobby and out into the street.

In front of the hotel there are two stone lions (or maybe they're just cement, I'm not sure) with their mouths open. As far back as I can remember, whenever Papa and Aunt Aurora and I went there to celebrate my birthday, which we did every year, I would steal two lumps of sugar and give one to each lion. When I was four or five I had to really work up my courage to stick my fingers in their mouths, and I was always very proud of myself for doing it. I had the sugar with me, but when we got outside I was afraid Mr. Potrezeski would think I was being childish, so I didn't feed them. Isn't that stupid? People shouldn't stop doing things because they're afraid of the way they look. He asked me if I wanted him to drive me home, but I said no. "I'm going to the shop first, and I like walking."

We shook hands. "I have no claim on your time," he said, "but we could keep in touch, don't you think? I enjoy walking, too, and we might take a walk sometime together."

"Yes," I said, and all of a sudden I felt like hugging him, for me and also for the young girl he used to watch in the garden, so I did. He was exactly my height. Probably, when he was growing up in Krakow, he had been much thinner. "Maybe I could come and see you before we go to Connecticut," I said.

"Excellent. You'll want to visit your property, in any event, now that you're a landlord, just to make certain I'm treating it well, though I assure you, you don't need to worry about that at all."

We were silent for a few seconds, and then I said goodbye and walked over to State Street. When I got almost to Jay Street I saw a woman and a little boy standing at the bus stop in front of the courthouse. They were facing the other way, but they looked from behind exactly like Fostra Lee Post and Claude. She had long blond hair and he had on a dark suit, and she wasn't paying any attention to him. She even pushed her hair back over both ears at once the way Mrs. Post did.

There were two stores near our shop that were open, but neither of them would cash a sixty-dollar check for me. At one place the manager told me he couldn't because it was a personal check from somebody who lived out of town, and at the other the manager wasn't in and the woman behind the counter said it was too large. The real reason, I knew, was that Papa had gone out of business, which made me mad, because Papa had really saved that street. Half the stores on it were still there only because he had gotten everybody organized and made it a place that customers wanted to come to and shop in. And now his daughter couldn't cash a sixty-dollar check there. It made me so mad I wanted to either cry or kick a pigeon. (Pigeons are the most kickable things in the world, the way they walk around as if they owned everything. They're like Uncle Shel with feathers.)

I went down the alley next to our shop and unlocked the back door. The same key fit the front door, but the lock in front was broken and you could only open that door from the inside. We always went in the back even before the lock was broken, because the burglar alarm on the front door had a ten-second delay and the one on the back door was set for fifteen, which is a big difference. I turned off the alarm and turned on the lights and bolted the door and looked around. There was always work to be done at the shop, even if it was just cleaning up. In fact, cleaning up was the most important work right then, because we wanted to sell the whole business in one piece, the presses, the building, the furniture, everything, and the cleaner and neater it looked, the more likely we were to get our price. We had gotten one offer the first week it was on the market, but it was too low. Now, according to the real-estate agent, someone else was interested, but you could never tell if anything was going to happen, so there was no use thinking about it.

After a while I went into Papa's office and sat at the desk and opened all the drawers, even though I already knew what was in them. I began to think about Phillip and how simple he had made his life. He wanted to get onto the football team in his sophomore year, so he did exercises and ran track and lifted weights. He wanted to be rich, so he worked and saved money and bought a sweatshirt that said *Harvard University* across the front. The running made him tired because of his fat, but that didn't really bother him. He probably liked being tired, and the sweatshirt covered everything.

I certainly didn't want to *be* Phillip Reinauer. I didn't

even want to be *like* him, but I didn't want to be like myself right then, either. At least Phillip had plans for what he wanted to do. I didn't have any plans except to leave Schenectady and go somewhere I'd never been and didn't know anything about. It was stupid. I wondered if Phillip ever wondered if he was being stupid.

Probably not.

I decided not to think about Phillip or me but to *do* something instead, something creative and original. I ended up doing four things:

1. I took three boxes of paper clips, containing 250 clips each, and made an enormous chain that I stretched back and forth across the office, to keep dangerous people from attacking me.
2. Just in case somebody came to the shop and wanted to play games, I took out a piece of paper and covered it with tick-tacktoe boxes.
3. I took out another piece of paper and wrote a letter to Mary Ellen on the typewriter. It said "Dear Mary Ellen, I have just taken a piece of paper out of Papa's desk drawer to write you a letter on. Love, Molly. P.S. In France, each elephant lady walks east in red drapes."
4. I took an envelope and wrote GET OUT OF SCHENECTADY EMERGENCY FUND across the front of it and put Mr. Potrezeski's check in it.

After that I was ready to leave, so I called home to tell them I was coming. Aunt Aurora answered and told me I didn't need to hurry because it was too late to help. She was mad, and I was embarrassed.

On the way I stopped at Kay's Drug Store and they cashed my check. They even let me have five dollars in change for phone calls, which I slid into one end of the envelope, which I folded over. When I got in the house it looked like somebody else's. Aunt Aurora had completely filled the downstairs with really good furniture from other people's attics. A lot of it, in fact, was better than the stuff we had sold. It showed how many people Aunt Aurora knew, probably people she had helped, because she was really a very good neighbor. She had measured each piece ahead so she knew exactly where to put it, so everything seemed to fit in. The house even smelled different.

Without saying a word to me, she handed me a rag and a can of paste wax and told me to polish the new dining-room table. Except for Claude, who was sitting on the front porch pulling the feathers out of an old sofa cushion and dropping them into the lilac bush, everybody was working, even Mrs. Post.

We ate dinner early, and afterward I told Claude that I would tell him a bedtime story if he let me put a bandage on his wrist. (His wrist was almost purple, and it was covered with little red pinhole cuts.) Ten minutes after dinner he came downstairs in his pajamas and held out his arm with his wrist up. Once for my birthday Papa gave me a homemade doctor kit. Mary Ellen and I used up the tape and Band-Aids in it in two days, but there were still some rolls of gauze in a box in the basement. I got it and wrapped the gauze all the way around his wrist, which was tiny, and taped it down with packing tape. It looked good and he was proud of it. I took him up to bed (he was sleeping on a cot in the sewing room over the porch) and told him a story about a good and handsome Prince who was locked up in a castle tower by a Wicked Usurper named Lord Blackheart. The Good Prince was only allowed to come downstairs at midnight, when a guard took him to the kitchen to get some watery soup and a dry doughnut. Lord Blackheart had a Good Daughter, who was also beautiful, and the Good Prince used to stand and look down at her through the bars of his tower window when she took walks in the castle garden.

One night the Good Daughter had a dream about a Good Prince who was locked in a high tower. The dream was so real that it woke her up and she couldn't go back to sleep, so she decided to go down to the kitchen and get some warm milk and honey. She tiptoed down the stone stairs, and when she walked into the kitchen she saw the Prince from her dream and his guard sitting at the table with a bowl of watery soup and a dry doughnut. She immediately fell in love with him, and for a few minutes they looked at each other while the guard scowled.

She decided to help the Good Prince escape by putting a special sleeping powder in her milk and honey and offering it to the guard, telling him that it was twenty-year-old Irish whiskey. He drank it and fell into a deep sleep, and the two lovers jumped on horses and rode away. The Wicked Usurper was so full of anger when he found out about the escape that he blew up bigger and bigger until he finally exploded, making such a bang that the two lovers could hear it even though they were already twenty miles away, and covering the walls of the castle with black, greasy goo. So they turned around and went back to the castle and married and became King and Queen and lived happily ever after.

Of course I stretched the story out when I was telling it, but Claude didn't mind. He wanted me to tell him another, and I said I would the next night if he kept the bandage on.

"I don't like it," he said. "I'm going to pull it off."

"O.K. I can't make you keep it on."

"You gonna tell me a story tomorrow?"

"Not if you pull it off."

"I'll tell my mother and she'll make you. She made you steal flowers and you didn't want to."

"That's right," I said, "but just because I was stupid today doesn't mean I'll be stupid tomorrow. Keep your bandage on all day tomorrow and I'll tell you a story that nobody in the world has ever heard before."

"I don't have to do what I don't want to do. My mother says that."

I kissed him on the forehead. "But your mother isn't the one who comes up and tells you stories."

Chapter 7

"**I**'m depending on you to be my bridesmaid," Aunt Aurora said when I came downstairs into the living room. "You won't let me down, now, will you?"

"No."

"Because Uncle Shel and I are having our wedding next week."

They were sitting on the couch together and I went over to her and hugged her and kissed her. I even kissed Uncle Shel. "Congratulations," I said, even though I didn't yet believe it.

Uncle Shel wiggled his mustache and smiled and nodded.

"Next Sunday afternoon at one o'clock at Saint John's Church," he said. "It's going to be a very small affair, with a luncheon afterwards for the family at the Van Dyke." He looked at Mrs. Post and winked. "Plus one friend," he said.

"We won't send out formal invitations," Aunt Aurora said. "I can invite the neighbors in person this week. It will give me a chance to tell them how nice their furniture looks."

I went and sat down on one of the new chairs and looked at Papa. Now there was really no reason to stay in Schenectady.

Uncle Shel cleared his throat and put on a very serious expression. "Sadly, my Uncle Lionel in Sussex has passed on," he said. "As you know, I'm his only heir. It means, of course, that I can at long last carry out my plans for the future."

Aunt Aurora waved her hand around. "At least I'm not leaving you with an empty house," she said, and then she looked at Mrs. Post and smiled. "And Fostra Lee is here just in time to give good advice to the bride."

Papa stood up. "We should have a party to celebrate. And entertainment. Fostra, do you sing, dance, or recite poetry?"

Mrs. Post smiled. "I can dance, but only with special music," she said.

"Well, Shelby will have to tell jokes then," Papa said. "And refreshments will arrive in a few minutes."

I got up and went into the kitchen with him. There was no time to bake a cake or make cookies, so we made cinnamon toast and I opened a can of pears and put them in bowls and broke up a Hershey Bar over them. While I was doing that I told Papa I thought he should go to Willimantic the next morning and see Mr. Ziesing about renting the printing shop.

"There are two Mr. Ziesings," he said.

"Well, you should go see both of them."

"Maybe I will."

We went in the living room and handed out the food, and instead of talking about the wedding we listened to Fostra Lee Post talking about Dr. Spiros Avanti, the founder of the Growth Channel Movement. It was as if he was God and she was engaged to him. "Just imagine, Dr. Avanti is going to be in the area in less than a week, *in person*, not by tape, for a whole afternoon and night. The average Growth Channel Assembly he addresses electronically, and even then he changes hundreds of lives. I heard him in person in January this year at a meeting in Tucson,

Arizona, and in one hour he taught me how to live. Since then I've read all his books, seen all his videotapes, listened to all his cassettes, and been to six in-person lectures in different parts of the country. He's brilliant. He has a Ph.D. in philosophy *and* a Ph.D. in psychology, he's only forty-five years old and he's already reached Life Track Eleven. He has the most advanced mind of the second half of this century."

"Who had the most advanced mind of the first half?" Papa asked.

Mrs. Post looked at him and smiled. "Mr. Theodore Morris, Spiros Avanti's uncle on his mother's side. He did the pioneer scientific researches from which Dr. Avanti drew his first axioms. He is still alive, and living in a small apartment in the Growth Channel Center in Sacramento, California, and he is a Track Twelve. Track Twelve is the highest track one can reach on the Earth Plane. You can't go any higher."

She went on talking like that until we finished eating and then she sent me upstairs to get a book called *Begin Living Today*. "I want you to read it," she said when I gave it to her. "You can keep it as a present from me. Bring it up to bed with you. All you need is to give it a chance to speak to you." On the front cover was a picture of Spiros Avanti standing outdoors somewhere. He had a gray mustache and lots of teeth, and he was wearing a golf shirt with a little flag on the pocket.

I told everybody it was time for me to go to bed and went back upstairs. When Papa came to say good night, I asked him again to please go to Willimantic soon and not think about taking any other kind of job until he did. "I don't want to stay in Schenectady, Papa," I said. "Now that Aunt Aurora's getting married, we don't have to."

He sat down on the edge of my cot. "There are a lot of benefits when you work for General Electric," he said.

"I don't want a lot of benefits. I guess I don't want to talk about it until after you've been to Connecticut."

"O.K., we won't."

"Papa, why isn't Uncle Shel going to his uncle's funeral?"

"Because it's long over."

"When was it?"

"I don't know. A few months ago, that's my guess."

"Then he knew he was going to be rich when he got you to buy him out. I'm going to ask him about that tomorrow morning."

"Don't. You're not sorry he left the business. He was a bad partner all along."

"I think he should at least admit that he lied to you when he said he was poor and got you to buy his part of the business."

"Why? Aunt Aurora is going to marry him in six days, no matter what. Why make her feel ashamed of him? She doesn't deserve that, and you don't need it. It's time to go to sleep."

"I want to talk another minute about leaving town."

"O.K., but only a minute. We have certain problems. You already know what they are. One, we have to sell the shop for a decent price. Two, we have to pay our bills. Three, we have to go on paying rent on this house through September when our lease runs out, no matter where we are. Four, the shop in Willimantic will cost money, which we will have to borrow. Five, Willimantic is a very small city. How much printing business is there? I don't know. Six, moving costs money, even when you don't own any furniture. But, seven, I'll go there tomorrow if I can."

"I just want to go someplace new, Papa. I don't want to

60

live here any more. Mama would want to start new, too, if she was here."

"Maybe, but she would make a good thing out of staying, too. Now go to sleep. Good night."

"Good night, Papa."

When I fell asleep I had a dream about Mama, only in the dream she was partly my mother and partly my sister, and we were almost the same age, though she was a little bit older, and we were living in the house in Krakow. We were getting ready for a party, trading jewelry and combs and other things back and forth, but not seeing each other. The maid carried everything from her room to mine and back.

I could hear Mama bumping around, opening and shutting drawers and going in and out of the closet, but I only saw her once, and then just for a second. She was all dressed and I wasn't and she handed me a pair of silver earrings as she went by the door. I saw her arm and her hair, and then I went out into the hall and saw her from behind turning the corner and starting downstairs. I stood there wishing she would come back up so that I could see her face, but I kept hearing her footsteps going down. Then she called to me, "Come on, Molly, there's all this dancing and you're not here yet." I went to the stairs and started down, and I went down faster and faster, and after a while I was sitting up in bed smiling and holding my ear, trying to put an earring through it. (I don't have pierced ears.) For a long time, sitting there, I could still hear the music. I didn't want to go back to sleep because the dream made me feel so good and I knew I couldn't get it back, but it was ten minutes to four and I was still tired, so I finally lay back down again. It was the first time in my life I had ever dreamed of my mother. Maybe I'll do it again sometime, as a wedding present or something.

I didn't wake up again until almost ten. I hate to wake up at ten on Mondays. Ten on Sundays is all right, but Monday is a workday. I also hate someone waking me up when I sleep late, especially if it's a stranger. But there was Fostra Lee Post sitting on my bed and looking down at me like the early bird watching a juicy worm. "I'm sorry to wake you up," she said, "but your father and I are about to leave for Connecticut, and we wanted to say goodbye." She leaned over and her hair swung down into my face. "I want to kiss you goodbye."

"You're going right now?" I asked her.

She sat up and shrugged her shoulders. "Your father doesn't waste any time," she said. "Didn't you ask him to go last night?"

"Right now?"

"Right now. He wants to see the printing shop he has his eye on. He said you thought it was a good idea for him to go. He called the people who own it and they said to come ahead."

"Oh," I said, and jumped out of the other side of the bed and started to dress.

"Will you watch out for Claude while we're gone?" she said. "He's in the back yard right now. You don't need to worry about him. He's as happy as a clam."

"I have to be working at the shop most of the day, cleaning it up," I said.

Mrs. Post smiled. She was wearing a white blouse and white jeans and tennis shoes. She looked perfect. "That's all right, Molly, I'm sure your aunt will watch him until you come back. Of course, she won't be as good at it as you are. You're a perfect role model for him. He looks up to you more than you would guess. And that's quite a compliment, because he has high standards in everything, so you should feel very proud. He won't be any trouble at all. Just one thing you need to remember. Don't let him have any matches. Fire is a very sensitive area with Claude right now. Goodbye. Have a fun day." She walked out.

I was barefoot, but I went downstairs right behind her. Papa was in the kitchen drinking coffee with Uncle Shel. (It bothered me to see him doing that, as if Uncle Shel was a friend of ours who had never done anything wrong to us, but Papa never stayed mad at anybody.)

"Hello, Molly," Papa said. "You look half asleep still."

"I'm awake. I had a wonderful dream about Mama last night. I'll tell it to you when you get home."

"You'll be asleep then, probably. I don't know how late we'll be. We might even stay somewhere overnight."

"O.K. Don't hurry if you get other things to do."

I sounded very calm, probably, but I was really upset and mad, not only at Fostra Lee Post but at Papa, too, because they were going away together for maybe a whole day and night and leaving me with Claude and Aunt Aurora. I was going to work while they had fun. I stayed in the kitchen until they left, and then I went upstairs and put my shoes on.

When I'm mad I either go for a run or I work like crazy, and either way I like to do it alone, so I got on my bike and told Aunt Aurora I'd be back in the afternoon and went down to the shop and cleaned machinery until about one o'clock. By then I was really hungry because I had been working hard and hadn't had any breakfast, but I didn't have any money to buy food with so I went over to the Carl Company and looked at wedding gowns. The saleswoman didn't believe me when I told her I was looking for a wedding gown for my aunt, who was exactly my size, but I didn't care. I knew it was the truth, so I looked.

When I got back to the shop, Phillip was standing at the back door with a worried look on his face. "I thought maybe you were dead in there," he said. "You may be dead when you get home. Your aunt's pretty mad at you. She said you left without eating breakfast and she called after you but you didn't pay any attention." He handed me a bag of lunch. "She said to give you this."

"I was in a hurry. Come on in if you want."

He locked his bike and I unlocked the door and we went inside. "Your aunt told me your father had pretty much decided to stay in Schenectady," he said.

"Well, she's wrong. We're going to Willimantic. There's a bookstore there with a printing shop next to it, and he's down there now talking to the people who own it. Do you want a sandwich?"

"Maybe just one. I'm only telling you what she told me."

"You mean she just came out and told you without you asking her?"

"She sounded pretty sure. If you do stay, you should try out for the cheerleaders. Carolyn Bassett didn't think she was going to make the squad last year, but she did. You probably could, too. You get to go to all the games."

"Cheerleaders are stupid."

Phillip shrugged his shoulders. "I gotta go," he said. He started to leave, and then he reached in his pocket and pulled out a can of Pepsi. "I forgot this. Sorry."

"That's all right," I said, and he left.

I sat there drinking my warm soda and thinking what I would do if I was a Linton High School cheerleader. Mess up, probably. There I would be with two minutes left in the big game of the season, Linton against Mont Pleasant on Thanksgiving Day, and the clock running down. The other girls and I are getting up. This is our last chance to cheer our team on to victory by spelling out the name of our beloved school. My "H" card is in my hand and I'm ready to go. We start bouncing up and down.

"Give me an L!"

"Give me an I!"

"Give me an N!"

Suddenly my glasses bounce off my nose. I get down on the ground and start crawling around looking for them. Now it's my turn to hold up my card, but I can't see to find it. The crowd gives a big cheer for LINTON HIG SCHOOL. Linton *Hig* School? Even the football players who can't read know they're not going to Linton Hig School. They're confused. They fumble the ball and Mont Pleasant recovers and runs for a touchdown. The game is over. We've lost. The coach comes over and tells me to leave Schenectady and never come back.

Sad story, except for the ending.

I finished my soda and cleaned machinery for another two hours, and by the time I left for home the shop really looked good. When I got home I was so hot (it's mostly uphill, riding home) that I put on my bathing suit and turned on the sprinkler in the back yard and walked under it. (I don't mind looking like a seven-year-old as long as I'm getting cool at the same time.) When Claude got home from the store with Aunt Aurora I tried to get him to come in, but he wouldn't do it because the water was too cold. I said he was probably too hot, and he said he wasn't, and I said he was, and we went back and forth like that for a while as if we were both eight years old.

Stupid.

Finally I stopped and sat under the sprinkler and

watched the grass while Claude sat on the back porch and watched me. "Your mother should buy you some summer clothes," I said after a while. "You've got a lot of underwear in your mother's suitcase, but you need shirts and shorts and a pair of sneakers."

"No, I don't," he said.

When I got up and went inside to dry off, I noticed that he didn't have his bandage on. I was glad, really, because it meant I didn't have to tell him a bedtime story.

It was just the three of us at dinner. (Uncle Shel was in Vermont picking up a new car that he had bought at a bargain price.) Aunt Aurora was still mad at me for missing breakfast, so she made a speech to me about how wrong I was to try to get Papa to leave town. "What your father needs now, young miss, is long-range security. And it's what you need, too. When I leave this house, that's two hundred dollars a month not coming in. Facts are facts, Molly. We can't always have what we want and just ride off and leave our troubles behind."

After dinner Claude disappeared for a long time and we really got worried about him. It turned out he was in the garage all the time and didn't feel like answering us when we called. While he was there he made a new bandage for his wrist out of rags and string, and when he came in he told me I would have to tell him a story, now. I did, but not until I had taken off his bandage and washed his wrist and put on a new one.

During the second story (Goldilocks and the Three Bears) he went to sleep.

I put on my pajamas and said good night to Aunt Aurora, who was waiting downstairs in case Uncle Shel came by, and went to bed. I was tired, but I kept listening for the sound of our car, so I got wider and wider awake. Around twelve the phone rang and I jumped out of bed and went

66

into the hall and listened to Aunt Aurora talking downstairs. It was Uncle Shel telling her that he wasn't going to come by the house on his way home. A little while later she came upstairs and went into her room.

To keep from thinking about Papa and Mrs. Post and listening for our car, I began to think about what I could give Aunt Aurora as a wedding present, and the more I thought about it, the more awake I got. Then suddenly I had a great idea. It was too late to print wedding invitations and send them out, but it wasn't too late to print wedding *announcements* that could be mailed out afterwards. Now that the handpress was clean and oiled, it would be so easy to set it up and run two hundred off. And it wouldn't cost me anything because I could take the cards out of stock.

Molly Smelter has great ideas.

No time like the present, especially for a really smart girl who doesn't mind riding her bike at night with no light. After all, the moon was out and there were streetlights. I had never done it before, but it was a lot better than going to the window every time I heard a car on Palmer Avenue, and feeling left all alone in the world, which I really wasn't.

I went out into the hall. Claude was breathing quietly and there was no light under Aunt Aurora's door, so the coast was clear. It's great to be awake when no one else is, unless you're sick. I went back in my room, got dressed, wrote a note to Papa telling him where I was and asking him to call me if he came home, put it on the bathroom mirror with a piece of tape that was left from Claude's bandage, and went and got my bike out. It was quiet outside, as if everyone in the world was asleep, and cool.

When I was very young, six or seven, Papa got me up in the middle of the night once because there was an enormous owl sitting in a tree across the street. He wrapped me in a blanket and carried me out onto the front porch and sat down on the steps with me on his lap. It was probably November, because there were no leaves on the trees and I was cold even in my blanket. There in the top of the Stenards' big maple tree was an enormous snow-white owl. After a while Papa went inside and made us two cups of cocoa and then took me back on his lap and we kept watching. Every once in a while the owl would slowly turn his head left or right. Then all of a sudden he was gone. Neither of us saw him fly away. He just wasn't there any more. We went on sitting and drinking our cocoa until it was all gone. I was sure that we were the only two people in the world awake.

Riding a bike at night was harder than I thought it would be, even with streetlights in most places. I tried to go slowly but it felt fast, and watching right in front of the front wheel for bumps made me dizzy. Before I got to Union Street I decided to go on the sidewalk whenever any cars came, so it took me almost twenty-five minutes to get to the shop, and halfway there I wished I had walked. On the other hand, I figured that if somebody chased me I'd be able to get away faster, unless they jumped out in front of me.

Once I was in the shop with the door bolted behind me, I felt completely safe. I put some water in the pot and put it on the hot plate to make some tea, and then I got to work. The small press was easy to handle and it was great to be able to do it and not get my hands filthy, so I purposely took my time. I didn't think about Papa or Mrs. Post or Claude or anything. When my first card didn't look exactly the way I wanted it to, I reset the whole thing in a different size, and this time my sample came out perfect, so I started making copies.

When I was through, I realized that somebody was turning the back doorknob, and that the only thing holding the door shut was the bolt. My heart jumped and started pounding and I just froze there staring at the doorknob turning back and forth. Then I saw that the slot holding the bolt was beginning to bend.

I shut my eyes for a second, and then I opened them and looked around. There was a big piece of wood under the photo-offset machine to put your feet on. I went and picked it up and walked slowly to the door. Halfway there, the board almost fell out of my hands, but I held on. When I got there I slammed it against the door as hard as I could. It sounded like a shotgun going off. It was so loud it hurt my ears. Before the echo of it had died away, I heard a car start and drive off. I sat down on the floor against the door with my feet out in front of me, shaking for a while until my heart started to slow down.

Then the phone rang. That made my heart jump, but after a second I realized it was probably Papa, so I got up as fast as I could and went into the office. My hands felt a little bit numb when I picked up the phone.

"Hello?"

"This is Sergeant Voorhees of the Schenectady Police. May I ask your name?"

"I'm Mary Smelter. I'm working here. This is my father's shop. I'm down here doing some printing work. Someone just tried to break in."

"If you would be so good, Miss Smelter, as to open the back door when you hear a knock, you will find two officers waiting to speak with you. There is a Mr. Bissel with them. He claims to be the owner of the premises and says someone recently discharged a gun in or near them."

"He doesn't own it. He used to own half of it, but he sold out to us. Nobody shot a gun."

"Well, he claims to own the premises. If you will just go and open the door when they knock, I'm sure you can work it out between you."

I said I'd go and open it, and then I realized that somebody was already knocking. I went to the door and slid back the bolt and opened it. Outside there were two policemen, one old and one young, and Uncle Shel.

"Hello," I said. "Is there anything I can do for you?"

Uncle Shel frowned and tried to look like an angry father. "Molly, what are you doing up so late? It's two o'clock in the morning."

"I'm working. Did you get your new car?"

"At two in the morning? Do you realize it's already Tuesday and you haven't gone to bed yet?"

"I was in bed before, but I have to get this job done by Sunday."

The old policeman took out his report book and asked me my name and address and phone number. "Do you often come here at night?"

"Only when I have a rush job."

Uncle Shel was still trying to look angry. "How can you have a rush job?" He looked at the policeman. "This place isn't in business any more. They don't print anything here any more, so how can she have a job to do?"

The policeman looked at me. "Is that true?"

"It's a personal job, and all the equipment works perfectly." I looked at Uncle Shel. "Does Papa know you still have a key?"

He tried to stand taller. "And who's looking after Claude?" he said. "His mother isn't home yet. I know because I just drove by your house. All the lights are out and the garage is empty. Aren't you supposed to be baby-sitting with Claude?"

"Does Papa know you still have a key?" I asked again.

The older policeman stopped writing and looked at him. "Do you have in your possession a key that you're not authorized to have?"

"I'm buying this business. I've already signed the purchase offer."

"Papa doesn't know that, does he?"

Uncle Shel shrugged. "I can't help it if he went off to Connecticut this morning. It's all cleared with the real-estate agent. What I want to know is who fired off that gun? That's why the police are here."

I shook my head. "I didn't hear a gun."

"I know a gun when I hear one go off, and I heard one go off right inside there," Uncle Shel said, pointing into the shop.

The young policeman stuck his head into the shop and sniffed the air and pulled it back. "I don't smell anything."

"I don't care," Uncle Shel said. "I know what a gun sounds like, and what I heard was a gun."

The older policeman looked at me. "Think back, Miss Smelter. Maybe you heard a shot and thought it was something else."

"I know for sure I didn't hear a shot," I said.

"You didn't hear a bang?" Uncle Shel said. "You must have heard a bang."

"I heard a lot of bangs," I said. "Every time you slide in a line of type it makes a bang. You know, Uncle Shel. It's a little bang, but it's a bang, sort of."

Uncle Shel put his fingers in his ears. "It was a rifle. It

went off practically right next to me. My ears are still ringing."

"At night everything sounds louder," the older policeman said. I could tell he didn't want to hear any more talk about gunshots. "Are you finished here, Miss Smelter? If you are, we could drive you home right away."

I looked at Uncle Shel. I didn't want to let him get into the shop without me there. "I really don't think anybody else should have a key," I said.

The policeman turned to Uncle Shel. "If you don't have the present owner's permission to enter the premises, you'd be safer to surrender that key for the time being. What do you think?"

Uncle Shel took out the key and gave it to me. "Thank you," I said.

The phone inside rang, and I went and picked it up. It was Papa to say he'd be right down to get me, but I told him that some very nice policemen were going to drive me home and I'd be there in ten minutes. When I got back to the door, Uncle Shel was already driving away in his new car. I reset the burglar alarm and turned off the lights and the policemen put my bike in the trunk of their car and took me home.

Papa met me on the porch, and before we went inside the house I told him about Uncle Shel signing a purchase order for the shop. He wasn't surprised.

Claude started making noises as soon as I opened the screen door, and I went upstairs and into his room. He was sitting up in bed shaking his head, shouting, "Don't come! Don't come!" The bandage I had put on his wrist was all unwound and hanging off and he was waving his arms around. I got close to him to hug him, but he banged me hard across the nose. (It was my fault for not thinking

about what I was doing. He didn't even know I was there.)
It hurt so much it almost made me cry. "You're safe at
home in bed," I said. "Everything's fine, there's nothing to
worry about."

My eyes were used to the dark by now, and I could see
his face clearly. His eyes were open, but he wasn't seeing
anything. I went into the bathroom and got a wet washcloth. When I came back, he was already starting to calm
down, but he was still shaking his head back and forth,
saying, "Don't come, don't come," very softly, as if he was
begging somebody. I took his hands and wiped them with
the washcloth, saying over and over again that everything
was all right and he didn't have anything to worry about.
His fingers felt puffy and dead. Then I gently washed his
face and after that I took him to the bathroom.

He was asleep almost before I got him back to his bed,
and I just sat there next to him for a while. His nightmare
was over. He looked so peaceful and far away, he was almost beautiful.

After a little while I realized that Papa was standing in
the doorway behind me. "Are you falling asleep?" he said.

"Halfway."

"Maybe it's time to go to bed."

"Probably."

I went to bed.

Chapter 8

When I went downstairs Tuesday morning, Aunt Aurora was on her knees cleaning the oven. I asked her if I could invite my old fourth-grade teacher, Miss Simmons, to the wedding.

"Why would you want to invite a grownup woman?" she said, still scrubbing away.

I wasn't sure. "I don't know. I like her," I said. "She's the best teacher I ever had. I'd ask Mary Ellen Cox, but she's in Philadelphia. I guess I just want somebody there who's my special guest. She's living in Saratoga, so she's not too far away."

"If you want to invite her, it's all right with me. Just make sure you call her after the rates go down."

"Thanks, Aunt Aurora. Where's Papa?"

"He's at the shop, and your Uncle Shel is with him. They have business."

I started wondering if Mrs. Post was with him, too, but then she came downstairs in her white satin dressing gown with the fur feathers down the front and went and got Claude out of the back yard and sat him in a chair and began talking to him about zoos and how wonderful it was to go to a place where there were animals from all over the world in one big happy family. "Wouldn't you like to spend a whole day at the zoo?" she said. "Don't you think that would be a wonderful adventure?"

Claude just sat there not saying anything.

"I can read what's in your heart," she said. "You'd love it, I can tell."

Claude still didn't answer, but he was beginning to look interested.

Mrs. Post began talking about how beautiful and graceful all animals were, especially giraffes. Then she stood up very slowly and made her neck two inches longer and began walking around the kitchen and making believe she was eating the top leaves off tall trees, stepping over Aunt Aurora's legs every time she passed the oven. Finally she sat down again and pulled Claude onto her lap and put her face against his ear. "Wouldn't it be wonderful to go to a place like that sometime?" she said.

He leaned his head back and looked at her. "Now?" he said.

She put a sad look on her face. "Not today, sweetheart, but sometime, and when that time comes, no matter who brings you there, you can run around as free as a bird. It's a shame. In fact it's *wrong*, but Schenectady doesn't have a zoo."

Claude's flat face looked blank again.

Mrs. Post frowned at me as if I was to blame for there being no zoo. "A city as big as Schenectady really *should* have a zoo, you know. Well, as Spiros Avanti teaches us, 'The big picture brings peace.' Schenectady certainly has a lot of things that Willimantic doesn't have. I can say that with certainty now because I've seen them both. But there's a wonderful park not far from here, and, Molly, I'll bet you'd love to take Claude there this afternoon."

I was amazed. I couldn't believe what I was hearing. "I can't go right now," I said. "I have to talk to Papa about something."

"About one-thirty? Right after lunch?"

"I don't know. It could be later."

"Well, I hope you and Claude won't waste the whole day sitting around here when you could be having fun. I would go to the park with you, but my friend Aurora and I are going downtown to find a dress that's good enough for her to get married in. Have you looked at that book by Dr. Avanti I gave you yet?"

"I haven't had time."

Mrs. Post leaned back and lifted her hair over her ears. "Just don't neglect it. It could change your life."

Uncle Shel drove his brand-new car into the driveway and got out and slammed the door and came in the kitchen and grinned at me. "I've been talking it over with your father," he said. "He'll be here in a minute. He's right behind me. He says he won't sell the shop to me unless you agree. I'm making a generous offer, and I'm sure you want to keep it in the family anyway. Did you get a look at my new car last night? It's in the driveway. I'm thirsty." He opened the refrigerator and took out Aunt Aurora's container of lemonade and grabbed a jelly glass from the cabinet. "I have great plans, including a few surprises. I love surprises. It's going to be one big happy family from now on." He looked at Fostra Lee Post. "You can join, if you'd like. Just marry her father."

I went out to the front porch to wait for Papa. When he came we sat down on the railing and he showed me Uncle Shel's purchase offer. "We won't get more from anyone else," he said. "I don't like to admit it, but it's a good offer. Uncle Shel has the money in the bank ready to transfer so there won't be any delay. We'll be free of major debts in under a week."

"And go to Willimantic?"

"You have a one-track mind."

"I just can't see staying here."

He shook his head. "Selling the shop and going away are two different things. But we can't even think about going away until it's sold."

"It's just I hate to see him get away with it, Papa. Everything seems so easy for him. It isn't fair. Still, we have to sell it."

"That's right."

"And it might as well be to him, I guess. He says he has a surprise for us."

"Do you have any idea what it is?"

"No, but I'd like to surprise him back."

We went inside and Papa signed the agreement on the kitchen table. So, except for the last official things, the shop wasn't ours any more. It made me feel sad.

After she was finished with the oven, Aunt Aurora packed a lunch for Claude and me and we went to the park. Neither of us said a word the whole way. When we got to the swings, I told him we were going to fly to the moon.

"I don't want to go," he said.

"Yes, you do. The moon is a great place. Uncle Shel isn't there." Claude looked at me as if he didn't know what I was talking about. I picked him up (he was very light) and put him on my lap so that we were facing each other, and we fastened our seat belts and pushed buttons and blasted off into outer space. On the way to the moon I told him about all the things we were seeing, and when we landed it was real bumpy, so he *almost* got afraid. After looking around the moon, we blasted off again and flew home and had another bumpy landing. He loved it and he wanted to go again right away. We made five trips, and after the fifth he still wanted more, but it was way after lunchtime and I was hungry and thirsty, so we went to the duck pond and ate.

After we were finished eating we fed the ducks sandwich bits and popcorn from the garbage cans. I told him that the park was really the Schenectady Zoo, and that the ducks were really tiny giraffes with feather suits on. "It's like your mother's white dressing gown, except that the duck suits have feathers all over them. You can tell they're giraffes by their long necks."

His eyes were very wide open. "They're ducks, they're ducks, they're ducks," he yelled, and then he ran away. At first I didn't want to chase him, but then I realized that he wasn't coming back, so I did.

"They're ducks," he screamed when I finally caught him. I was mad at him for running away, but he looked so afraid that I felt even more sorry for him. "Sure they're ducks," I said. "They came out of real duck eggs laid by real mother ducks, and all their relatives are ducks. I was just making a stupid joke. You want to go back and count their relatives and see how many there are?"

"No."

"You want to go get a doughnut?"

"No."

"Then let's go home and see what kind of a wedding gown your mother and my aunt have bought."

It turned out to be an ugly pinkish tan, with dark-brown lace around the middle. I'd call it an old lady's dress, except that I don't want to insult old ladies. Mrs. Post must have known it was ugly and wanted it that way. I don't know why. All the way through dinner she talked about how hard it was to find just the perfect dress, and how lucky they were after a lot of searching to have found it. I wondered what she was going to wear. Something white, probably. I went upstairs and stayed there until time to set the table.

Sometimes you do things that you haven't thought about doing, so when you do them you're surprised. After dinner I got out my Get-out-of-Schenectady Emergency Fund and went to the phone booth near Kay's Drug Store and called Miss Simmons in Saratoga and asked her if I could come up and see her soon. She asked me when, and I said tomorrow, and she said wonderful and maybe we could go to the ballet at the Performing Arts Center. "Wednesday is a good night, usually," she said. "Do you like ballet? Thursday would be just as good for me."

"No, I'd like tomorrow. Also, Thursday I'm supposed to go to a meeting with the woman who's visiting us."

"I think you'll like it. How will you get here?"

"By bus, and then I'm sure Papa will come and pick me up."

"Fine."

We said goodbye, and I decided that since I was going to Saratoga I'd see Mr. Potrezeski. I called him at home and said I'd be there around twelve. (I didn't know what the bus schedule was, but I figured there *had* to be a bus that would get me there on time.)

"We'll have lunch if you're free," he said.

"Yes, that would be nice. I'd like to ask you about what kind of place for business Willimantic, Connecticut, is. You know, Papa and I might move there. Is there any way you could find out about it before tomorrow?"

"I could perhaps discover a few things."

"I'd also like to know about the Ziesing Brothers' Book Emporium. How long they've been in business and how they're doing and things like that."

"I'll find out what I can."

"Thank you very much. That's very nice of you. Well, I'll see you tomorrow."

"I look forward to it. We'll have a picnic lunch."

We said goodbye and I hung up and then I stood in the booth for a few minutes thinking. I had forgotten to invite Miss Simmons to the wedding, and instead I had ended up inviting myself to Saratoga. I wasn't sorry, but it wasn't what I had expected to do. I put another dime in the phone and dialed home, hoping Papa would be the one who answered. He was, and I told him I had invited myself to Saratoga to see Miss Simmons the next day, and asked him if he could pick me up there at night. He said sure, that it was a good idea because I needed a day off. (I didn't tell him about also going to see Mr. Potrezeski. I was a little ashamed of keeping it a secret, but that didn't stop me.)

"Are you alone?" I said.

"Everybody's out for a ride in Uncle Shel's new car."

"Then can we talk?"

"Sure."

I sat down on the sidewalk under the phone. "It's funny, isn't it, all of a sudden being surrounded by rich people. Uncle Shel and Mrs. Post, anyway, and Aunt Aurora is about to marry money."

"I don't know if you'd call Mrs. Post rich in the same way Uncle Shel is. She gets a check every month from Mr. Ralph Dixie Post, but that doesn't make her rich. I think she spends it all on airplane tickets."

"Her ex-husband's middle name is Dixie?"

"That's what Aunt Aurora says. He's living in Mexico with a dancer."

"If Mrs. Post gets fresh money every month, why doesn't she buy Claude some summer clothes so he doesn't have to wear those heavy things and sweat all the time?"

"She's too busy following the Life Energy along her Growth Channel."

"Do you believe that, Papa?"

"I don't even know what it means."

"I thought she was going to leave Friday, but I guess now she'll probably stay for the wedding."

"Probably. If you're going to Saratoga tomorrow, why don't you come home now and get to bed?"

"I promised Claude a bedtime story. Did you notice if he still had his bandage on?"

"Tonight I'll tell him a story. You need rest."

"O.K., Papa, I'll come home. See you in five minutes."

On my way home I thought about Miss Simmons and realized why I had wanted to see her and why I wanted her to be there at the wedding. I wanted to have somebody like my mother to protect me from Fostra Lee Post. I don't know what worried me about Mrs. Post, but I was really afraid of her. She was like a child nobody had ever said no to, and who didn't care what she did as long as she got what she wanted.

I didn't go to sleep right away. I got some candles and shut the door and read. (The book was *Emma*, by Jane Austen. It's a long book, but it's wonderful once you get into it.) I heard everybody come in about eleven, and about eleven-thirty I went into the bathroom to get ready to go to sleep. I looked down out of the bathroom window and saw Claude lighting matches in the back yard. I watched him for a minute, and then I went downstairs very quietly and out the back door and watched him from the back porch. I should have gone over to him and picked him up right away, or at least called to him, but I wanted to see exactly what he was trying to do.

He was sort of curled up around a little pile of newspapers and sticks. There was a wind, so his matches kept going out, but he kept lighting new ones. I made a few noises, but he was so concentrated on his work that he didn't notice me. I couldn't believe what I was seeing. It was after eleven-thirty and here was this skinny eight-year-old boy playing with matches in my back yard. Every time he struck a match his flat face lit up for a second and his eyes glittered. He looked as if he was hypnotized. He took more matches out of his pocket and began lighting them, leaning way over the paper. All of a sudden the paper caught fire and a second later his shirt was burning, too. I yelled and jumped off the porch. He heard me and looked up, but by that time I was already on top of him. He still didn't know that his shirt was on fire, because it was hanging away from him and it was all mixed up with the fire from the paper. I grabbed him and hugged him against my stomach, and then he felt the burn. He pulled back and kicked and wiggled, and since the fire was out and he was really hurting me, I let him go. When he hit the ground he almost fell down, but then he bounced and sort of danced around for a second and ran for the street. I ran after him down the driveway. When he got to the street he tried to open the door to Uncle Shel's car and then he turned around and ran back, almost crashing into me. By this time Papa was out in the back yard and Claude ran right into his arms. The porch light was on and I could see Claude's face over Papa's shoulder. It was completely white and his eyes looked twice their normal size. He was screaming. I could smell burned cloth. I thought it was from Claude, but then I looked down and saw that I was smelling my own pajama top.

By that time, Aunt Aurora was running water in the kitchen to make some strong tea to put on the burn, and Mrs. Post was holding Papa's arm and telling Claude that he should be happy because he was going through a wonderful learning experience and Uncle Shel was telling everybody good night because he had to go. I went around to the front of the house and upstairs and took off my pajama top, which really stank. On my stomach there was a circle of red dots which stung a little but really weren't serious burns. I looked in one of the boxes of clothes and pulled out another pair of pajamas and put them on. It wasn't cold, but I was shivering a little.

When I came out of my room Papa and Claude were in the bathroom. His shirt and undershirt were lying on the floor near the door and he was sitting on the edge of the tub. His undershirt had a brown circle on it about the size of a pancake and Claude's chest had a red circle on it exactly the same size. Aunt Aurora came upstairs with a measuring cup with strong iced tea in it and handed it to me. "Get some cotton out of the closet there, and sponge it on him." (It really helps. You put six tea bags in a cup of boiling water, and then when it's strong enough you put ice cubes in it to cool it. The tannic acid in the tea is good for the burns, and of course it feels good.) Papa took off the rest of Claude's clothes and the two of us washed him down while Mrs. Post stood at the bathroom door telling all three of us how wonderful it was to have new experiences in your life.

When Claude was clean and finished with his tea treatment and in his pajamas, I carried him to his bed. As long as I sat next to him and kept talking he was calm, but as soon as I stopped he would start to wiggle around and bounce up and down. When I finally told him it was time to go to sleep he jumped out of bed and ran into the bathroom, climbed into the bathtub and started playing with the drainplug, pulling it out and putting it back in as fast as he could. I was afraid he was going to turn on the water, and I didn't want him to do that because he only had one pair of pajamas. I got him back in bed by promising to tell him a story. "You'll have to lie still and listen," I said, "and not move," so he pulled the sheet up to his neck and got completely stiff, which looked a little weird.

I told him the story of my mother's life from the time she was a baby until the night she ran away from Krakow. Most of it I made up, but some of it I remembered from stories Papa had told me. I even remembered some things I had forgotten, like the fact that on her seventh birthday all three of her uncles brought her teddy bears. I added some romance by telling about a handsome young man who lived secretly in the attic and on her tenth birthday sneaked into her bedroom in the middle of the night and left her a dozen roses with a note saying, "With love from your Secret Admirer."

When I finished I slowly stood up, thinking that he was asleep, but he opened his eyes and started to wiggle, so I sat back down and talked to him about fire. I thought that maybe if we talked about it he would get his worries out into the open. (Molly Smelter, girl shrink.)

"Do you know why fire burns?" I said.

"From matches."

"Well, yes, but do you know why matches burn?"

"From when you strike them."

"Matches burn because the air mixes very fast with the cardboard in the match. If a fire has no air, it goes out. That's the reason I picked you up and hugged you before, to get the air away from the fire."

"You hurt me," he said. He was rubbing his wrist again, and for about ten seconds I thought he was going to swing at me.

84

"Your shirt was on fire," I said. "I grabbed you so no air would get to it, and the fire would go out. Playing with matches is dangerous."

"My mother says it's all right."

"Do you agree with her? It was your shirt that caught on fire. Do you think that playing with matches is a wonderful experience?"

He didn't answer, and I pulled up my pajama top and showed him the burn around my belly button. "I don't think it is," I said. He looked at my burn and didn't say anything, and then he pushed the sheet away and slowly pulled up his pajama top. His circle was a little bigger than mine, but it wasn't as red. "Did you see the flame fly up when I hugged you?" I said. "It flew in front of my face and I heard a little snapping noise."

He didn't say a thing, but he sat up and started to push his stomach out toward mine. I pushed mine out until we were touching. He was ticklish there and he started giggling and pretty soon we were touching stomachs back and forth and I was giggling, too, even though it hurt a little bit. (It probably hurt him, too.)

The only way I could get him to lie down after that was to promise to tell him another story. I told him the story of Cinderella. It was the first time he had ever heard it. (I was amazed. Here was a child eight years old and he had never heard even the name of Cinderella. How can anybody in the Western world get to be eight and not know it? Amazing. I had never heard about tennis until I was eight, because Papa and I didn't start playing until then, but you're almost *born* knowing who Cinderella is.) It was fun telling the story to somebody who had never heard it before, and when I kissed him good night I promised to tell him the story of Snow White and the Seven Dwarfs the next night. "I know about Snow White," he said, "except that I can't remember the end."

I kissed him again. "Don't sleep with your face flat on the pillow, Claude. We're going to make that a rule from now on."

When I left his room I didn't want to see anybody again, at least for a half an hour. I went to the bathroom and locked the door and just stood there thinking with the light off. I was sorry I had kissed him good night and promised him that story. I didn't want him to begin to like me or expect anything from me. The more I was nice to Claude, the more I was trapping myself. And what good did it do him, since he was going to be going away? The more he liked me, the more he would miss me.

The top half of our bathroom window was green glass so that people couldn't see in. (The bottom half had a curtain.) All night the street light shone in and the whole room looked slightly green, as if it was under water. I took off my clothes and started the bath running and sat down on the bath mat in front of the mirror on the door and looked at myself for a long time, stretching and bending and counting my ribs and seeing how I looked sideways and backwards. Then I moved closer to the mirror and carefully examined every part of myself, seeing how my toes wiggled and how my knees bent and how my legs connected with my body and how long I could make my neck. (Not as long as Mrs. Post when she was a giraffe.)

When the tub was full I looked at the water and got the temperature just right and decided I was too tired to get in, so I went to bed and had a dream about Claude. He and I were going to the Greyhound Station together because he had to catch a bus to Texas and I had to get him there on time. On our way there were things we had to pick up and deliver, and we had to do it by walking on boards from roof to roof. Every once in a while I would look down and see the bus station between the buildings, but we never got close to it, even though we were sometimes down in the street. There was a policeman on a motorcycle parked on a board between two roofs, and we had to climb over the motorcycle all the time. The policeman didn't seem to mind, but it bothered me that he might suddenly ask us what we were doing.

The dream went on and on, and it was always almost time for the bus to leave, and we never got to it.

Chapter 9

The next morning at breakfast, while Papa and I were talking about how late he should pick me up in Saratoga, all of a sudden Claude threw his toast on the floor, turned over half a glass of orange juice, pulled off his T shirt, ripping it on purpose, knocked over his chair, and just stood there staring at the table. At first I thought that maybe the burn was bothering him, but he didn't even look at it. "Get the sponge out of the sink and wipe up the orange juice," I said, but he just stood there, and after a minute he turned around and ran outside.

Mrs. Post got up and went to the door and looked out at him. After a while she came back to the table and sat down again and smiled. "Isn't it wonderful how Claude has learned to express his true inner feelings?" she said. "If all of us could be free and open in our self-expression, it would be a better, happier world."

Nobody answered her, partly because of the noise that was coming from the back yard. Claude had picked up a whole lot of stones from around the rosebushes and was throwing them at the garage wall, making a terrific banging noise. Aunt Aurora got up and went out to the back porch, and I followed her to see what she was going to do. Claude heard the door opening and closing and looked at us for a second with a rock in his hand, and then he turned away and threw it at the garage. Aunt Aurora walked down

88

the back stairs and went and stood in front of him. "People on Palmer Avenue, no matter what age they are, don't do that, and you won't either," she said. "You will replace the stones where you found them and you will return to the house."

She turned around and came back into the kitchen and sat down at the table again. It's funny how you can live with somebody for a long time and then suddenly see something that you never saw before. That happened to me at that moment. For the first time in my life I could imagine her as a mother and not just an aunt. After a minute Claude came in and got the sponge from the sink and began to wipe up the table, even though it was already clean. While I was watching him I decided that I was going to make Aunt Aurora's wedding bouquet, if she let me. I also remembered my wedding announcements, that were still lying next to the small press, if Uncle Shel hadn't thrown them away.

It was getting late, so I excused myself and went upstairs to get dressed to go downtown and catch the bus for Saratoga. When I was almost done, Mrs. Post came into my room and stood there in her white dressing gown with a little box in her hand. "I want you to have this as a gift," she said. I sat down on my cot and opened it up. It was a long pearl necklace made out of very small pearls, with a small silver clasp she called a frog. I knew right away that the pearls were real.

She twirled them around my neck three times and clipped the frog together and took a mirror out of her pocket so that I could look at them. She was trying to buy me, and I knew it, but she also sincerely wanted me to have the necklace, and I never say no to a present, anyway, so I said thank you and got my shoes to put on. (I've always loved presents, no matter what they are. It doesn't make any difference to me whether they're beautiful or ugly. I think that when somebody gives you something, you shouldn't take away that person's pleasure by saying that they shouldn't have done it or you can't take it or something like that.) I was wearing my best dress, which was white with small blue flowers on it (in fact, the dress was also a little small, but that's something else), and the pearls went with it perfectly.

Mrs. Post sat down on my cot and began telling me how wonderful Schenectady was and how great it was to grow up in one place and really have roots. "Why would anyone want to leave here?" she said. "It's such a wonderful place to develop your potential in. If Schenectady was my home, I'd *never* leave it, at least not until I was fully grown." She got up and looked out of the window and told me how lucky I was to be starting high school in the same place where I had gone to kindergarten. And all the time she talked about Schenectady she kept putting in things about me, how wonderful I was, and how much she had learned from me, and how I was bound to grow up to be a wonderful woman. I felt I ought to break in and tell her that she was wonderful, too, but I couldn't because I didn't believe it. It's one thing to lie about presents, even when you don't like them, and another thing to lie about people's characters.

She stopped talking and kept looking at the front yard. I looked out, too, and there was Papa playing ball with Claude. For some reason that made me remember Aunt Aurora's wedding bouquet, so I told Mrs. Post I had to go, and ran downstairs. When I got to the bottom I turned around and went back up and got my Get-out-of-Schenectady Emergency Fund from under my pillow (fortunately,

Mrs. Post was out of the room) and ran back down again. Aunt Aurora was finishing the dishes.

"Aunt Aurora?" I said.

"Your father's in the front yard," she said.

"I know. I wanted to ask you something. Would you like me to make your wedding bouquet? I'd consider it an honor, and I'd try to do a really good job."

She looked down at her hands and then back at me. "It's very kind of you to make the offer," she said.

"You could tell me exactly how you wanted it to look," I said.

She began to put away the dishes. "It's a very nice idea, but I've already ordered a bouquet, and Uncle Shel has paid for it."

I was really sorry. "I'd like to do whatever I can to help with the wedding," I said. "I printed some announcements a few nights ago that you might like to use. Uncle Shel could pick them up. They're in the shop. Also, I want you to know that I think you were great with Claude before."

Without thinking about it, I went over to her and kissed her. She was surprised, but I think it really made her happy. It made me happy, anyway. "You've already said you're going to be my Maiden of Honor, Molly," she said, "and I'm depending on you. We'll have to go and find something for you to wear. We'll go to the Carl Company tomorrow or Saturday."

I told her whatever she wanted to do was fine with me, and kissed her again and left. This time she kissed me back. (I'm sure she must have kissed me when I was a baby, but I can't remember it, so in a way this was the first time. I don't know why we wait so long to do things like that.)

I went downtown in a hurry because I wanted to stop on the way and give the lions at the Van Dyke the sugar I still owed them from Sunday, and I had to be at the Greyhound station by 10:25. I fed the lions and got to the station in plenty of time, and even after I had bought my ticket I still had more than forty dollars left in my fund.

When the bus was pulling out of the station I saw Phillip Reinauer walking across State Street holding hands with Carolyn Bassett, so I spent the first half of the trip feeling really mad, which was stupid. Phillip was too old for me, and I always knew that, and he was also too young for me. In a way he was like a five-year-old and a fifty-year-old. Still, when you think somebody's in love with you it feels good and you get to depend on it, in a way. What bothered me the most was that the person he was giving me up for was my age and a klutz. She smoked, she cheated on exams, and she always had the latest thing on. I had lunch the same period, and she used to walk through the cafeteria very slowly every day wearing something new and tight. She had a very large brassiere and a very small brain, which I guess is what some guys like.

About halfway to Saratoga I decided that I should be glad about it because it was another reason for me to want to get out of Schenectady. Even if I wanted to stay, I couldn't say any more that Phillip needed me or would miss me.

When I got to Saratoga I went straight to Mr. Potrezeski's office, which was on the second floor of a building two blocks from the bus station. I was a little nervous, but he was so glad to see me and so nice that I got over it right away. I thought maybe the dollhouse would be in his office, but it wasn't. On his office door, in gold letters, was *Walter Potrezeski, Investment Counselor*. Very impressive.

He had a big leather chair in front of his desk, and I sat in it while he told me what he had found out about Willimantic. "It's a small city in eastern Connecticut, which you know."

"That's all I know," I said.

"Well, the city has a decent credit rating. The downtown is being redeveloped, which is true in urban locations of every size. Downtown property is only moderately expensive. The main business is a thread company. The Ziesing Brothers' Book Emporium is owned by two brothers, Mark and Michael Ziesing. It's financially sound. They pay their bills. It's the only true bookstore in that part of the state. You have to go to Boston to find one as good. The printing business next door was operating until two years ago when the owner died. The Ziesings bought the building, and they want it used. Now, if I may offer advice, I must say that long consideration should be given before you go into business in a strange city. It is very risky, *very* risky."

"That's what my aunt thinks, too."

"Your aunt has good sense. General Electric is hiring again. Did you know that?"

"Yes, Papa's been there."

"Is there a place for him? Has he been offered a position?"

"Not yet, but he will be, probably."

"He should consider it seriously."

"I guess so." I tried not to let him see it, but I really felt terrible. Everybody in the world wanted to get Papa to work for G.E. I didn't really expect Mr. Potrezeski to tell me that Papa should go to Willimantic, but I was hoping for something close to it so I could go home and tell him that my investment counselor thought it was a good idea. Now, if I said anything, I would have to say that he thought it was risky.

"Shall I show you Saratoga?" Mr. Potrezeski asked.

"Yes, that would be fun," I said.

We went all over the place, including the race track, and ended up in front of the library at Skidmore College. "I would like you to know," he said after a minute of looking at the building, "that I would be delighted to meet any expenses that might be beyond your means when it comes time for you to go to college. I would be prepared, if that were appropriate, to cover all of your expenses."

"Thank you very much," I said. "I expect to work part-time, so I probably will be all right."

We got out of the car and he took a picnic basket out of the trunk and spread a blanket right there on the lawn. "If someone objects, we'll tell them you're looking over the college with the future in mind," he said.

The food was great, and when we were having cake he took out two packages. One was a framed picture of Krakow, looking down from the top of a church, so you could see all the streets and the country around it. The other was an album of photographs of my mother and her family. "I took these when I left the house in 1946 to go to the West," he said. "I had no right to them, naturally, but I felt as if I was the last member of the family, in a manner of speaking, and I knew that if I didn't take them they would be lost. These are the originals, but I've had very good copies made for myself, so I'm not losing anything by parting with them. You don't mind my having copies, do you?"

"No. You should. You have a right."

"No. With you I have no rights, only privileges."

There were twenty-three pictures. Seven of them were just of Mama alone, and most of the others had her in them. One picture had my grandfather and four other men, all in business suits, sitting around a table in the garden. Somebody, and Mr. Potrezeski and I were both pretty sure it was Mama, was standing behind the dining-room window. It was just a shadow, but it was the right size. Mr. Potrezeski pointed to my grandfather. "Without him, I would be dead," he said.

There was a picture of Mama at her tenth-birthday party. At least there were ten candles on her cake, plus a big one in the middle. Another picture showed the whole back of the house in the morning with the family (plus an uncle or somebody) having breakfast outside. You could see the window of the attic hideout room. You couldn't see anything behind the window, but I'll bet he was up there when the picture was snapped, standing behind the copper strip and looking down. The best picture was a close-up of Mama sitting in a chair with a crown of flowers in her hair. She had her head turned just the way it was in the painting over the fireplace in the dollhouse.

It was wonderful to get those pictures, and I thanked him probably ten times. "They're yours," he said. "I should have given them to you long ago, except that I couldn't resist watching you in secret for a little while. You'll have to forgive me for that."

"May I ask you one more business question?" I said when we were putting the picnic basket back in the car.

"Certainly."

"How much is the dollhouse worth? I just want to know. I don't want to sell it."

"Between two and three hundred dollars."

"Thank you."

"You thought it would be more?"

"A little more." (Actually, I was thinking it might be worth a thousand dollars, or maybe just a little bit less.)

"Someone with a personal interest or connection would be willing to pay more, of course."

"I don't want to sell it," I said. "I just wondered."

We went back to his house, and I called Miss Simmons from there. While I was waiting for her I looked at the dollhouse, which was in his hall on a table, with lights inside. He hadn't put any lamps in, but there were four or five bulbs hidden in different places so that it looked like a house at night. "I can take the lights out when my lease is up," he said, but I just told him that it looked beautiful, which was true.

After a few minutes, Miss Simmons came. I was afraid Mr. Potrezeski would want to kiss me goodbye (which would have been all right, now that I think about it), but he didn't. We shook hands like old business partners and I said I would call him again soon.

It was great to see Miss Simmons, and during almost the whole time I was with her I didn't think about money or business or moving out of Schenectady. She looked exactly the same. She had a long, bony face with almost no lines in it, and gray eyes, and a very soft voice. Also, she had beautiful hands. When I was in her class and she was looking over my shoulder at something, she would sometimes put her hand on the back of my neck and rub it a little bit. It wasn't just me she did that to, she did it to everybody who liked it. She had perfect handwriting, and she could stand at the blackboard and be looking at you and be writing at the same time with her left hand. I guess she was really showing off a little bit, but it really was amazing.

I had never seen her anywhere else but in school, but still it didn't feel funny riding in a car with her. (She was so much a part of school that when you stayed after to water the plants or something, you'd see her take off her glasses and pinch her nose and look around the empty room as if she was surprised that everyone was gone. That was another thing I liked about her, that she had wire-rimmed glasses just like mine. In fact, I think I got wire rims because of her.)

We went to her house and then for a long walk, just looking at different kinds of trees and wild flowers. I only mentioned Willimantic once, and she told me she had a cousin she visited sometimes in Ashford, which was about fifteen miles away. We went out for dinner in a restaurant, and then to the ballet, which I had never seen before. Actually, it wasn't one ballet, it was three, two short ones and a long one.

During intermission, while we stood out on the lawn watching the sunset, she told me about becoming a teacher after she had been out working for the telephone company for fifteen years. "I had a good job and I was working with people I liked, but there are times in your life when you have to give up one good thing for the sake of something better," she said, and then she told me what it was like to be starting college at the age of thirty-six. She had to pass gym, for instance, and learn how to swim or they wouldn't let her graduate.

While we were talking I suddenly saw how beautiful she was. I don't mean that she was beautiful for a person her age, but that she was just beautiful. It was partly her voice and partly the way she stood but mostly her eyes, though she also had a great figure. She looked the way Mama would have looked if she had lived to be fifty.

When we got back to her house after the ballet, Papa was waiting on the porch for us. She asked him to come in for a cup of coffee and some cake, and while we were sitting at her kitchen table I started talking about Claude. I told her everything bad I could think of about him, which wasn't hard. I didn't stop talking for ten minutes, and when she asked me about his mother I talked some more, though not quite as long. The fire, the rocks, the business about the zoo, the way he rubbed his wrist, and everything else that bothered me came out. It felt good, but then at the end I also felt embarrassed because I had been telling on somebody. "It's probably not as bad as I make it sound," I said.

"It sounds bad enough to me," Miss Simmons said. "I'm just surprised you weren't complaining about them all afternoon. I think that shows great self-control and maturity."

I knew she was just saying that to make me feel better, but it worked.

On the way home I told Papa about Mr. Potrezeski and the pictures, but I didn't tell him what he had said about Willimantic. He wanted to see the pictures right away, and he stopped and turned on the light inside the car so he could. The fact is, I almost kept the pictures a secret, too. I don't know why. Maybe I wanted to own my own private fairy godfather or something.

Chapter 10

When we got home, Fostra Lee Post was waiting in the living room wearing her white satin dressing gown with the furry feathers down the front. Aunt Aurora was upstairs in bed and Claude was on the couch asleep in his clothes. It was one-thirty in the morning, but I stayed downstairs because I didn't want to leave Papa and Mrs. Post alone.

She was sitting in the chair under the lamp sewing two big circles of yellow velvet together around the edges. The velvet was getting all bunched up, and even though she was only halfway around I could see that there was no way she could make it come out even at the end. "It's going to be a smiling sun," she said. "It looks a little unfinished right now, but later I'm going to turn it inside out and stuff it with foam rubber and then all the rough places will be smooth."

"If you're going to sew the face on, you probably should do it before you go the rest of the way around," I said.

She looked at me and kept on stitching. "I'm going to cut the eyes and mouth out of green felt and put them on with Elmer's glue. It's creative, it isn't something to use. Of course I also want him to be able to rest his head on it whenever he wants. I'll tell him to be kind to it. If you have a conception of something in your mind, like the concept of a Love Pillow, then you will find a way to realize it. That's a key Growth Channel concept, and it never fails. It can't fail. If you have an idea, it's bound to come true. For instance, tonight Mr. Avanti's executive assistant called and said that Mr. Avanti wanted me to be the Chief of the Volunteer Facilitators on the text desk tomorrow night."

She rolled her sewing up into a ball and sat there hugging it and smiling and wiggling around like a girl waiting to try out for the cheerleaders. If she had jumped up and done three cartwheels and a split, I wouldn't have been surprised.

"What is a Facilitator?" Papa asked.

"It's a person who is deeply into the Movement who helps newcomers to choose the right Growth Channel literature for their stage of development. You'll understand better tomorrow night. Then you'll see clearly why Growth Channel is the *one true answer* for everyone in the world who wants true personal growth."

Aunt Aurora came downstairs and into the living room in her old blue terry-cloth robe. Mrs. Post didn't even look at her. "Did I ever tell you about Spiros Avanti's private secretary?" she said. "Two years ago she was just an ordinary woman in New York, and now she's a completely new person with a completely new personality. Spiros Avanti turns you completely inside out, like this Love Pillow. There's a place for everybody. There's a big place for young people. In fact, there's a separate young people's club. It's called the Growth Groovers. Isn't that a *now* name? It's just for kids like your beautiful daughter. It has its own newsletter and national officers and local meetings and everything. I'll bet there's a Growth Groover Group at your school right now, Molly, and you don't even know about it."

"I never heard of one."

She put her hand on my arm. "Even a smart girl like

you can miss things, you know. And if your school doesn't have one yet, you can start one. You're a born leader, and it's right down your alley."

"I'm not sure," I said, but she wasn't listening.

"Right now I don't want to have to think about anything else but focusing my energy. Truly, I don't ever want to think of anything else. A member of Dr. Avanti's staff will aid the volunteers by speaking to us at four in the afternoon, and then Dr. Avanti will put the final touches on us before we go to our posts. Shelby says he'll drive me to Albany, so now everything's arranged, and the world is perfect for me."

"How will he do it?" I asked.

"In his new car."

"I'm sorry, I meant how will Dr. Avanti put on the final touches?"

She looked at me as if she thought I had suddenly turned really stupid. "He'll *focus our energy*. That's one of his many many gifts, getting people into the right Channel and helping them to stay there, and that includes young people. I just told you about the Growth Groovers, didn't I? Once you see them you'll love them. Claude loves them already, even though he's a *little* bit young. And of course Claude loves you, as you know. Whenever he's with you, he's as happy as a clam. I can tell from the way he looks."

"Excuse me, I have to go to bed now," I said, and went upstairs.

Chapter 11

Right after breakfast Thursday morning Aunt Aurora
went to work in the garden and Uncle Shel started
asking Papa questions about how to get the business started
again. He had a big pile of pamphlets about new equipment,
and he wanted Papa's advice about what to buy. Papa
answered questions for about ten minutes and then he
picked up all the pamphlets and put them on the sink and
sat back down again. "I want to ask you a question," he said.
"When did your uncle die?"

"Uncle Lionel?"

"Yes."

"Last March or April. By the time I found out, the
funeral was over. That's why I didn't go."

"Could he have died in February?"

Uncle Shel looked down at his hands. "Now that you say
February, I think it probably was February. I didn't know
how much money I was getting until much later, though.
That's why I didn't say anything to anybody. I wanted to
be absolutely sure of exactly where I stood and exactly how
much the inheritance was going to be. And you know how
the British are when it comes to money, Harold."

"No, I don't. How are they?"

"Well, I don't know either," Uncle Shel said, "and that of
course is exactly the problem."

Papa leaned forward. "Shelby, Molly and I have been going through some difficulties since the business went broke. If we had known about your money and your plans to buy the place even a month ago, we would have worried less and had more time to play tennis."

Uncle Shel smiled. "You can believe me, Harold, all this is going to work out for the best."

"Molly and I have been uncertain about how we were going to pay our debts since March," he said. "Perhaps that isn't a long time, but it has *felt* like a long time."

"You may not believe this," Uncle Shel said, "but I've spent a lot of sleepless nights worrying about what you were going through. But you have to understand, all that's over and behind us. In three days I'm going to be an official member of the family, and after that I'm going to do you a lot of good, and I'll admit, I probably owe it to you."

Papa shook his head. "The only thing you owe us, Shelby, is the truth. We feel we have a right to that. Molly and I are about to go to the park and play tennis, but while the three of us are alone together, tell us the truth. When you told me in March that you were poor, you knew that you would soon be rich, isn't that true?"

"Well, I didn't exactly know it."

"Shelby, you're lying."

"Well, I was pretty sure."

"You weren't pretty sure you were in for a lot of money, Shelby. You knew."

He grinned a stupid grin. "Well, I guess so."

Without another word, Papa and I got our tennis rackets and went to the park. On the way he told me how he knew that Uncle Shel's uncle had died in February. "He bought me lunch on February 17 to celebrate my birthday," Papa said, "and Uncle Shel only buys people lunch on days that he inherits large sums of money."

"Papa, have you decided yet if we're going to Willimantic?"

He put his hand on my arm and we stopped walking. "I haven't decided to go to work for General Electric or anybody else," he said. "G.E. hasn't even offered me a job yet, though they probably will. There are a lot of benefits to working there. Medical insurance is one, and if I stay twenty years I can retire with a steady income. If I get sick, or when I get old and can't work, I won't have to depend on you to pay my bills."

"I don't care about those things."

"You're not forty-four years old and the father of an interesting daughter, so you don't have to, but I do. I don't want to be foolish now and make us both pay for my foolishness later."

"I'd rather have you poor and old and foolish than rich and living here. I mean that."

"I know you do, but you're not thinking ahead."

"I just want to be free and start all over again someplace new."

"Why?"

"I don't know, but it's not just for myself. It's also for you, Papa."

Papa nodded. "I know that, Molly." We started walking along again, and I thought about telling him that he didn't have to worry about me because Mr. Potrezeski would give me money for college, but I decided not to because I didn't think it would help.

I'm not a completely bad tennis player. I have a terrible dink-ball serve, but my forehand is fair and my backhand works sometimes and I'm fairly fast. I bought a book summer before last on how to improve your game, and Mary Ellen and I really studied it and practiced all the time I wasn't working and the courts were free, and we won the girls twelve-and-under tennis tournament that year. (The next year two girls who had been taking private lessons at the Mohawk Country Club beat us.) When everything is going right for me I can outplay my father.

I beat him 6/4, 2/6, 6/4. (My backhand was terrible in the middle set, and he was serving very hard.) After we got home, I took my Get-out-of-Schenectady Fund and went back down to Union Street and called Miss Simmons in Saratoga to find out if she was going to Ashford any time soon to see her cousin, and ask if I could come along. She said she wouldn't be going again until September or October because her cousin, who was also a teacher, was in Colorado working for the summer. I said "Oh," or something like that, and then I remembered to ask her to the wedding on Sunday. She said she was sorry but she couldn't come, and I said it wasn't important and I hoped to see her again soon. I didn't start to cry until after I had hung up the phone.

When I got home, Mrs. Post and Claude were sitting on the front porch steps waiting for me. She had promised him that as soon as I got back from wherever I was the three of us would go to the park and swing and then go eat lunch out. "I can't," I said. "I have a very important letter to write, and then I have to take it to the post office to mail it, and after that I have some other important things I have to do."

I went straight upstairs and into my room and shut the door. In fact, I didn't have to write a letter, but to keep from being a liar I sat down and wrote a short letter with a complicated P.S. It took me about a half an hour.

July 13

Dear Mary Ellen,
    Are you still alive?

Love,

Molly

P.S. Some cool heroes enter New England contests (tenis) and dumbly yell insults. Superior ball-game organizers, rejecting insults, naturally go north or west.

I put it in an envelope and addressed it and took it to the post office, going out the back door so Mrs. Post and Claude wouldn't ask to go with me. After I mailed it I called the Connecticut Information Operator and got the number of the Ziesing Brothers' Book Emporium and dialed it.

"Ziesings' Book Emporium."

"Hello, this is Molly Smelter. You know my father. He was there looking at the printing shop a few days ago."

"Oh yes. How can I help you?"

"Is the shop sold yet?"

"No."

"We're thinking about buying it. Did my father talk to you about holding it for us while we thought about it?"

"No, not that I recall, and we could only do that if you gave us a deposit."

"Well, can you tell me if there are any other people interested?"

"Other people have looked at it. I don't know how interested they are."

"But if we put down a deposit, that would hold it?"

"For sixty days."

"How much would the deposit have to be."

"Five hundred dollars."

"I see. This may sound silly, but I wonder, are there tennis courts in Willimantic?"

"You mean public ones?"

"In a park or somewhere."

"There are two that the city runs, and then there are some at the high school."

"How many?"

"I don't know. Maybe eight."

"So altogether there are ten?"

"About."

"Thank you very much."

"Is there anything you want to know about the shop while you've got me on the phone? I think your father pretty well covered it, but we might have left out a few things."

"No, thank you. Maybe I'll call back later. Thank you very much."

I hung up the phone. Five hundred dollars was five times more than I thought he would say. But I liked the sound of his voice. It sounded really friendly.

When I got home Mrs. Post and Claude were in the living room dancing to the music inside Mrs. Post's head. She was saying "One-two-three, one-two-three, one-two-three," and he was trying to copy the steps she was doing. It was hard for him because she was just stepping around and sideways and bending him over backwards every once in a while.

"Come on in and we'll make a threesome," she said, but I told her I had to go right back out again.

She stopped dancing and looked sad. "You said we were going to the park, and now I'm sad. I feel like throwing stones at the garage."

"It was you who said we were going to the park, Mrs. Post," I said.

She smiled. "Well, I guess you're probably right. But we will have a chance to talk before I leave for Albany, I hope. There are some things I really need to say to you before I go."

I went on into the kitchen and told Papa I was going to Linton and run around the track and I'd be back in a little while. As I left I heard Aunt Aurora telling him that running was bad for girls. I didn't wait to find out what he said back.

I must have really felt left alone right then, because my main reason for going to Linton was to see Phillip and talk to him. He was there, running around the track. The second time around running next to him I invited him to the wedding.

"Can't come," he said.

"Why not? It won't take long. It's at one o'clock. It'll be over by two."

"Can't."

We were coming out of a curve and he started doing a wind sprint down the straightaway. I stayed right with him. (He was a lot heavier and fatter than I was, so there was no way he could outrun me.) We went around the next curve and did another wind sprint together, and then he stopped and stood there puffing.

"I really am sorry," he said.

"I'm just sorry you're going to have to miss it. It should be nice, if you like weddings."

"I'm sorry, too."

"What are you going to do?"

"Go up to Sacandaga."

"Somebody's house?"

"The Bassetts have a big place there."

"Oh."

"They asked me a long time ago."

"Did Carolyn like the poem?"

"I don't know. I haven't shown it to her yet. I'll probably keep it. I just showed it to you because you've got good taste. I have to do some sit-ups now, and then I have to run some more."

"That's O.K. I have to go home anyway."

I left him sitting up and puffing and went home very slowly. When I got there, Mrs. Post was on the front porch with Uncle Shel, waiting for me. She told Uncle Shel to get in his car and start the air conditioner going, and then she took me across the street. "I love you and trust you," she said.

I just stood there. It's embarrassing when somebody tells you something like that and you don't feel the same way.

"I'm so glad you're coming tonight," she said. "I know the assembly will give you something you can keep for the rest of your life. Everything in your life will be completely different after tonight. Believe me, I know."

I nodded as if I believed her. (It turned out that she was telling the truth.)

"Are you looking forward to the meeting?"

"Yes, I am."

"For my sake, but also for Claude's sake, I'm glad we've met and shared so much. Claude has never known somebody like you before, and he and I are both richer for it." She suddenly grabbed me and kissed me on the mouth, and then she pulled back and examined me. "Did you ever think of getting fitted for contacts? Contact lenses, I mean, instead of glasses."

"No. My friend Mary Ellen got them, but they kept swimming on her eyes. That's what the doctor called it."

"That wouldn't happen to you unless you wanted it to.

You should try them. They're well worth the extra money. Well, the car is cool by now, so it's time for me to go." She turned around and walked across the street and jumped into the car, and Uncle Shel drove off. I stood watching the car until it turned left at the end of Palmer Avenue. I even waved, because that's what Mrs. Post was doing.

Aunt Aurora and I spent the rest of the afternoon on the porch with her recipe file. Papa was at the bank and I didn't even think about Claude. We went over the recipes one by one, and every one that I liked or I knew Papa liked we copied down on a card, so that I would have a file of my own after Aunt Aurora was gone.

When we were about halfway through the file we heard something moving under the porch. There was a lot of loose wood piled down there, and some pipes left from when the house was built, so at first we thought it was a cat knocking things over, but then Claude's finger came up through a knothole in the floor. Aunt Aurora called down and told him to come out right away. He just pulled his finger back and didn't answer. Then she said something in a loud voice about all the splinters and rusty nails under there, but he didn't move, so she went around to the side and bent down and offered him cookies and lemonade if he would come out. She even said she would bake him a cake from her best recipe, orange spice cake, but he was silent.

I went around and got down next to her and asked Claude if he had seen a cat at any time while he was under there. "He's a gray cat with black stripes," I said. "Have you seen him? His name is Admiral Benbow, and he belongs to the Greenes down the street. He's a perfectly nice cat. He wouldn't hurt a fly, but he's lost." (I was telling the truth. Admiral Benbow was one of the nicest cats I have ever known, and he had been missing for over a year.)

After a few seconds Claude said, "I don't see him. He's not here."

"Are you sure? Look around."

"I don't see any cat."

"Well, look around again and see if there's a person there in a cat suit. Naturally, it would be a midget. Also, he'd meow in a funny way."

"No."

"Well, if you happen to meet something down there in the next few days that looks like a cat, go up to it and ask it to play Chinese checkers. If it sits down and says it wants firsties, it's Captain Benbow. If it lets you go first, it's the midget."

"I don't know how to play Chinese checkers."

"He'll teach you, or if you want to come out, I'll do it now. I have an old set in a secret hiding place in the basement."

Aunt Aurora and I went back onto the porch and started to work again, and two minutes later Claude came up. "Show me," he said, so I told him to help Aunt Aurora while I went down to the basement and got out the old Chinese-checkers set. I took my time, and when I came back, Aunt Aurora was trying to teach him how to put the recipes back in the box in alphabetical order. The trouble was, he only knew two letters, C and P, and he didn't know which came first. She kept acting as if he had just forgotten it temporarily, but then she took the cards away from him. "What do they teach you in school in California?" she said.

"I don't go to school."

"You don't go to school now because it's summer-vacation time, but when you're in school, don't they teach you letters and numbers?"

"I don't go to school. My mother says I don't have to."

Aunt Aurora looked at him and then at me and then back

at him. "If you don't go to school, you'll never learn to read and write."

"I can read and write, but my mother says I don't need to yet."

Aunt Aurora got up and took the recipes inside, and I stayed on the porch with Claude and played Chinese checkers. He learned very fast.

Chapter 12

The first part of the meeting that night was boring, but after God came out in his brown-and-white shoes, his gray suit with the silver threads running through it, his red silk tie, and his diamond pinky ring, it got interesting. Spiros Avanti was really a great speaker. He'd be serious for a few minutes, and then all of a sudden he'd be funny, and then he'd just stop talking and look around the room. His speech didn't seem to be planned out at all. It was as if he was thinking it all up on the spur of the moment. And his jokes were never on other people, they were always on himself.

We arrived at the motel more than a half hour early, but the auditorium was already almost full. We found five seats together near the back, and then Claude and I went to look for Mrs. Post. She was in the lobby selling books, but there were so many people around her table we couldn't even get close. She was wearing a red skirt and a white blouse and a little plaid hat and she had a big smile on her face. All the female Growth Channel workers were dressed the same way. The men, including Dr. Avanti's Chief of Staff, wore sky-blue slacks and navy-blue blazers with light- and dark-blue striped ties.

The first thing that happened was that the Field Co-ordinator came out and welcomed everyone and introduced the Growth Groover Life Singers, who sang. They were high-school kids, with maybe a few college kids thrown in, and they all looked like people in a Coke commercial, snapping their fingers and bouncing around and looking happy, which I guess is what they were supposed to do. They all wore white cheerleader sweaters with G. G. on the front in red. After a while one of the guys got a chair and put one foot up on it and played the guitar and sang a solo while all the others hummed in the background. Aside from that, their singing and music weren't bad.

After they were finished some of them gave little speeches. Really, they gave the same speech over and over again. "I used to be a loser, and unhappy, and without any friends, and on the wrong path, but now I'm a winner, and I'm happy, and I have friends, and a wonderful future." The last person to talk was the solo singer. He asked all the teenagers in the audience to raise their hands if they wanted to be happy. I didn't raise my hand and not many other people did, either. In fact, there weren't many teenagers there. There were a lot of adults old enough to have teenage children, but I guess they had left them home.

God's Chief of Staff came on stage then. He had the same smile the kids had, and he told us what great young people the Growth Groovers were and got them out again for another bow and more applause. I applauded because I felt sorry for them. When the applause died down the Chief of Staff told us how his life had been completely changed by Spiros Avanti. "I won't stand up here and tell you I'm a new man," he said, "because I'm much more than that. I'm a *different kind of being* from the one I was before I became a part of the movement, and you can be, too. It's easy."

He went on talking for about twenty minutes, and then, when everybody was getting completely bored, he introduced Spiros Avanti, who came out on stage and talked for an hour, which seemed like fifteen minutes. "Find your special Growth Channel and follow it wherever it leads," he said over and over again. "People will tell you you're selfish, but can it be selfish to want back what others have taken away from you? *You belong to yourself.* In your hand are the seven keys to unlock the seven locks of life."

For each of the seven keys he had a story, and they were all really the same story. Somebody unhappy comes to the Growth Channel Movement and becomes happy and free and has more money. He made it sound easy and fun.

Most of the time he was talking, Claude was wiggling. I didn't want to take him out of the auditorium because I was really enjoying Dr. Avanti, but I felt sorry for him, so about halfway through the speech I got a pencil from Papa and taught him how to play tic-tac-toe on the back of the program. After all, it wasn't his fault he was there. He was only eight years old, and he probably had heard the same speech lots of times all over the country. And also he was hot, wearing his blue wool suit.

When God had finished his speech he came down from the platform. His helpers passed out pamphlets about a Growth Channel Personal Development Weekend, and he gave a commercial for it. He said it was going to be "two days that will change your life, for only $250 per person, plus room and meals." He really made it sound like a big bargain. Then he told us what a wonderful meeting this one had been, and everybody applauded him, and he applauded everybody back, and he left and people started to get up and wander around.

Across from the registration desk downstairs there were display cases for different businesses in the area, and I took Claude down there to look while we waited for his mother to be through. In one case there were a whole bunch of ball bearings and gears turning around, and Claude and I stood and watched them for a few minutes. Then all of a sudden three Growth Groovers came up behind us and started to talk to us. I think the group had split up with orders to find every teenager they could and get her or him to join.

"My name is Barbara," the tallest one said, "and this is Carol and this is Gary. Who are you and where are you from?"

"Molly Smelter. I'm from Schenectady, but I'm moving away in less than a month."

Barbara gave a sweet smile. "Maybe you'll decide it's better here. Anyway, I'm from Schenectady too, and I go to Linton. Is that where you go?"

"I'm moving to Connecticut."

"You could still change your life tonight, before you go."

"It's already changed. I'm a different person completely from what I used to be. Really, I'm completely different."

Gary squeezed his head between Barbara and Carol. "What do you mean you're completely different?"

"Claude and I didn't used to be the way we are now. We used to have webbed feet. Isn't that right, Claude?"

All three of them took a quick look at our feet. Unfortunately, we had shoes on. "You mean you had to have an operation?" Gary said.

"No, we were born that way, but we got tired of swimming around and eating popcorn and worms."

Gary pulled his head back, and Carol started to look around for other teenagers, and Barbara said they had to go, so they went.

"It wasn't so much the feet," I said as they were walking away. "It was really the feathers that bothered us the most." Gary turned around, but all three of them kept walking, and after we had gone around and looked at the rest of the cases, Claude and I went back to the auditorium.

Papa was standing in the aisle talking to Aunt Aurora,

but he immediately sat down, so that he and Claude would be on the same level. "Your mother is going to stay here for a while and do some more work. She has a ride home, and she wants us to go ahead."

Claude didn't seem surprised or say anything. He fell asleep almost as soon as we got in the car, and Papa and I started talking about Dr. Avanti. "He's dangerous," Papa said.

"He didn't *act* dangerous," I said.

"Anybody who never laughs at himself is dangerous."

"He told stories on himself a lot."

"No, he didn't. He told stories about the way he *used* to be. That's easy. He never let us laugh at the way he is *now*. Now he knows all the answers. Now he's found the true way. Now he follows it absolutely, and you should, too. That's what he wants you to believe, and that's dangerous. Be free by doing exactly what he says."

Claude sat up in the back seat, wide awake, and Papa stopped and bought us all ice-cream cones. When we started driving again I asked Papa if he could remember the seven keys for the seven locks of life, and Claude started to recite them. It turned out that he knew them by heart, and he could rattle them off like a machine. It was creepy.

We went to bed right after we got home, and when I woke up, it was still dark and I could hear rain. Mrs. Post was sitting on my bed. Her hair was in my face, and it was wet.

"Molly, are you awake?"

"Yes."

"Are you awake enough to talk?"

"Yes."

"Can we go downstairs?"

"Sure."

"I have a lot to share with you."

I wanted to know what time it was, but I didn't want to ask her, so before I went in the living room I went and looked at the kitchen clock. It was eight minutes to three. When I came into the living room Mrs. Post was on the sofa. I sat down in the big chair under the lamp. "It's raining," she said, "but I think it's stopping."

"When we came home it was smelling like rain," I said. "I guess we really need it, it's been so dry."

She swayed back and forth and shut her eyes as if she was going to get sick, but then she opened her eyes and looked at me. "Key four says you must be conscious of your feelings at every moment," she said. "And you must be ready to express them to others and follow where they lead. I need to express my feelings to you."

I just sat there.

"Did you like the meeting, Molly?"

"It was very interesting."

"Did your father like it?"

"He thought it was interesting, too."

"Molly, when I love someone with my whole being, I sometimes write that person a letter to express my deep feelings, because it's more personal, sometimes, than saying them. See that letter on the table? I wrote it because of the deep feelings I have for you and my son. That's my letter to him. You'll have to read it to him because he has trouble with big words. If I wasn't so full of feelings right now, I'd wake him up and read it to him myself. Are you warm enough?"

"No."

"Go get a robe. I can wait."

I ran upstairs. I didn't want to go into Papa's room and wake him up, but I purposely made noise opening my closet, hoping he'd hear me and get up. He didn't, so after standing in the hall for a minute I went back downstairs, putting on my robe as I went. Then I sat back down on the chair, with my feet folded under me, and waited.

"It was a wonderful meeting, wasn't it? I'll bet it wasn't what you expected, was it? Dr. Avanti can lift up a whole room of people and turn them completely around. But a word to the wise. You have a lot of growing to do, and plenty of time to do it in. You don't have to make a decision right now. Stay where you are and weigh everything carefully."

I didn't know what she was talking about. She was beginning to look a little bit sick again. "Would you like a cup of tea?"

"No, thank you. You're a wonderful girl. Everybody at the meeting was deeply moved and overcome. He gets better and better. You could see that. But that's not really what I wanted to talk to you about. I had a vision tonight. Did you ever have a vision? Well, it's not important. I'm sure you believe in them. Joan of Arc had visions. Perhaps all of us have visions, but most of us deny them out of fear." She leaned back and smiled and patted the pillow next to her. "I saw you growing up right here, in this house, putting down roots and drawing nourishment from them."

"I've lived in Schenectady all my life," I said.

"That's what I mean. Well, I've done all the talking so far, and you probably want to say some things. I just want to say, first of all, what a wonderful boy Claude is, I mean what a wonderful person he is, and how wonderful it is for him to be here in this house with you."

"It's a nice house," I said, and she repeated the word "nice" and said I was exactly right, that "nice" was the right word. Then all of a sudden she started talking about Spiros

Avanti again, and then she stopped and looked at her watch. "You have to forgive me. Dr. Avanti and Claude are the only two important men in my life, so I concentrate on them. And your father, too, of course, who could help it? You're very lucky to have a father like that. But you must know that, don't you?"

I didn't want to talk about Papa. "Did you know that the only letters Claude knows are C and P?" I said.

She took a deep breath and pushed her hair back behind her ears with both hands. "First things first, Molly. He knows the Seven Keys, which is more important in the long run. It's not what you *know*, it's how you *feel* that counts. Still, reading and writing and arithmetic are important in their own way. Did you go to school in this neighborhood when you were growing up?"

"At the Hillside School. It's only about three blocks away."

"Is it a good school?"

"Yes."

"Claude ought to go to a school like that someday. I remember where it is now. Your father and I walked around the outside of it Monday or Tuesday morning. I have a deep gut feeling about the Hillside School being right for Claude. What do you think? No, I won't ask you what you think. It's after three in the morning, which is no time to ask a girl anything. I'm going to write you a letter to tell you my feelings. You don't mind that I got you up, do you? You can go back to sleep."

"I don't mind."

She came over to me and put her face against mine. Her cheek felt very hot, as if she had a fever. "We understand each other, don't we? We may not always feel exactly the same way about things, but we really understand each other."

120

She stepped back and I stood up. The rain had made her hair curl a little bit around her forehead. She looked very pale, and I thought maybe she was going to faint. "Everything's going to be all right," I said.

"Oh yes," she said. "That's exactly right. I feel exactly the same way. I have this gut feeling about it. You go on up. I'll come up, too, in a few minutes."

I went back to bed and woke up again at six, when I heard Phillip bang out his door to start on his paper route. (He was half an hour late.) I was just about to shut my eyes again when I saw an envelope on the floor with MOLLY written across the top of it in big letters with lipstick. I got up and read it.

Darling Molly,
   The letter to Claude is in one of your tennis shoes. Please read it to him when you think best. I'm on my way to California. Tonight was one of the most beautiful nights of my life—in part because of you! I don't have the heart to wake Claude up, but I'll kiss him goodbye. What a wonderful memory to treasure!
                                        Love always,
                                        F.L.S.

P.S.   I'm leaving you a gift. It will be in the glove compartment of your father's car. It's something I won't need any more!

I read the letter four or five times, and then I got the letter to Claude out of my tennis shoe and sat down on my bed and read it.

My Darling Claude,
   Be happy! Starting right now, your Mother is beginning to use *all* the Seven Keys of Life. Someday, I know you will do the same thing, and that will make me very happy. It's such a

wonderful thing to finally know the Channel of your True Self.

I'll be in Sacramento part of the time, growing and working under Dr. Avanti. So you see how things can work out when you keep trying and never give up.

I'm very happy because I know I'm leaving you in good hands. From the first moment, I knew that Molly was a person I could trust, and now that you belong to her family you must trust her, too. Won't that be fun? Your mother has your best interests in her heart all the time!

Remember always, even when I'm not with you in the body, that I'm with you in spirit. Soon you will get another letter from me and a package with a Love Pillow in it that I'm making for you with my own hands. Won't you be excited to get it?

Love always,

Your loving Mommie

P.S.   I borrowed Mr. Smelter's car. Tell him that it is in the parking lot at Albany airport, and say thank you to him. Always be polite!

P.P.S.   Remember when you used to call me Dockie and I used to call you Budgie? It's such fun when you have secrets together, like we do!

In the envelope with the letter was a bankbook with Claude's name and mine on it. Mrs. Post had opened an account for us on Monday, July 10. There was $1,000 in it.

I put the letter back in the envelope and went downstairs and sat on the porch and tried to think. I wasn't surprised at all. I was mad and worried, but I wasn't surprised. Going to California was exactly what she would do. She had been setting me up for it since the night she came.

Chapter 13

After a while I came inside and went to Claude's room and just stood there looking at him for a long time. His knees were pulled up almost to his chin and his face looked calm and peaceful and happy. What could I do for him? What was he going to do to me?

Sometimes when I have a big problem I just stop thinking and get paralyzed. That happened to me while I was watching Claude. For a while it was as if I couldn't move. Finally I told myself that I had to get dressed, and then I was all right. After I was dressed I picked up the letters and went to Papa's door and slowly opened it. He was awake, reading.

"Mrs. Post is gone," I said. "She took off to California. She left one letter I'm supposed to read to Claude and another one to me. She's not coming back."

He closed his book. "Come sit on the bed. Are those the letters?"

I handed them to him. "She says she's going to California and from now on we're his family. She's not coming back. She doesn't say that exactly, but I know. She woke me up in the middle of the night and brought me downstairs. It was crazy. There's a bankbook in the envelope with a thousand dollars in it."

"In Claude's name?"

"His and mine."

He read both letters, the one to me first, and then he handed them back. "We could get the police after her for desertion."

"Could we?"

"Probably. She's deserted her son. There ought to be a law against that."

"Do you think we should?"

"I haven't thought about it. I don't think it would help Claude. It might help her. Do you like him?"

"No."

"Neither do I."

"He can't help his face, but he's really mean sometimes."

"We need to talk it over with somebody neutral. Why don't you call up Miss Simmons, tell her what happened, and say we want to come up to Saratoga today and get some good advice. We need to talk to somebody outside the family who has some feeling for children. There's a picnic grounds at Saratoga Lake."

"Would we take Claude?"

"We can't leave him with Aunt Aurora on the day before her wedding eve. Besides, Miss Simmons should meet him. Try not to wake him up for a while. We'll do it when we're almost ready to go. Just tell him his mother isn't here. He's used to that. We don't have to read him the letter right away. Tell Miss Simmons we'll try to get there around twelve. Uncle Shel will have to drive us to the airport. I just hope we don't have to spend two hours finding our car. Are you all right?"

"I'm beginning to feel better."

"Things always look better when you've made a few decisions, even if they're only for the next few hours. Now I'm going to shave and get dressed. It's a good day for a picnic by the shores of Saratoga Lake. I'll make the sandwiches. It's my turn."

I went downstairs right away. Uncle Shel was sitting in the kitchen waiting for Aunt Aurora to come down and make him breakfast. I didn't want him listening, but our only phone was in the kitchen, and he was going to find out about Mrs. Post pretty soon anyway, so I dialed Miss Simmons's number and told her what had happened. "I don't know if I can help," she said, "but I'll be glad to talk about it and meet Claude. Just don't forget to bring your bathing suit in all the excitement."

"We'll buy Claude one on the way up," I said. "Which reminds me, we'll also need some suntan lotion or something. His skin's been covered up all summer and he's as white as a sheet."

When I hung up, Uncle Shel pointed his finger at me and nodded as if he'd known all along what Fostra Lee Post was going to do. "When a woman starts moving around like she has, it's bound to happen sooner or later. Look at me. I've stayed in Schenectady all my life and I've done pretty well. In fact, I've done *very* well, and I haven't gone flying off to California. But let's face it, women are more likely to do something like that."

"Excuse me, Uncle Shel," I said. "I have to go upstairs."

"Just one minute, I have to talk to you. It'll just take a minute."

"Really, I have to talk to Aunt Aurora."

"It can wait. This'll just take a minute. I want you to know that you're wrong about me holding grudges. I would never hold a grudge, especially against somebody who was going to be my niece-in-law."

"I never thought about you holding a grudge against anybody."

He shook his head and grinned. "I know better," he said.

"Really, Uncle Shel, I have to go upstairs. And I don't know what you're talking about."

He pointed his finger at me again. "Because of that night," he said. "Come on, don't pretend. You remember."

"What night?"

"At the shop, with the police. You didn't know then that it was my shop. I understand."

"It wasn't your shop."

"Not technically, but practically."

"I had a right to be there, Uncle Shel. You stopped me from finishing a job I was doing." He had walked around and was blocking the kitchen door, so I went out the back and around the house and in through the front. I passed Papa coming down the stairs. "Aunt Aurora's up, but she's getting dressed," he said. "I haven't told her yet."

I knocked on Aunt Aurora's door and went in and told her about Mrs. Post leaving. At first she didn't believe me, even though she could see that Mrs. Post hadn't slept in her bed. "Her clothes are still here," she said. "Fostra's playing a joke. She wouldn't leave her son." I gave her the letters and she read them, and then she handed them back to me as if they had poison on them. "People don't do that," she said.

"I couldn't believe it at first, either," I said. It was a lie, but I didn't want her to feel alone.

She shook her head. "I never knew her. I just never knew her at all," she said, and got up and went downstairs to make breakfast.

I went into Claude's room and told him that his mother was away and that we were going on a picnic at the lake.

He didn't say anything.

"Did you hear me?"

"I don't like picnics."

"Well, you'll like this one. Breakfast is in five minutes. Get dressed and I'll carry you down piggyback."

During breakfast Aunt Aurora kept looking at Claude in a sad kind of way, but he didn't notice. To keep him from thinking about his mother, I talked to him about different things we might do on the way to Saratoga and after we got there. I found out that he didn't want to buy a bathing suit, or swim or wade or get his feet wet, or eat sandwiches, or drink soda, or meet Miss Simmons, or go on a boat unless I let him do all the rowing and steering.

"If we rent a boat," I said, "you can row part of the time and look for fish the other part of the time."

"I want to row and look for fish all the time," he said.

Papa stood up and looked at Claude. "The first thing we're going to do is play a game called 'Find the Car.' Here's how you play. One person goes to a large parking lot, like one at an airport, and parks your car, and you go there a few hours later and try to find it. It's fun. When he's finished breakfast in a few minutes, Uncle Shel is going to drive us to the airport in his new car so we can play."

It turned out that the car was next to the entrance gate, but we purposely went right by and gave Claude clues so that he would be the one to find it. When we got in the car I wanted to look in the glove compartment to see what Mrs. Post had left me, but I waited until we stopped and Papa had taken Claude into a store to buy a swimming suit. It was her wristwatch. I didn't touch it. It's still in the glove compartment, as far as I know, under the maps and behind a screwdriver.

Miss Simmons was waiting for us when we got to the lake, and we went right to the beach. Claude wouldn't put on his swimming suit, but that was all right, because he also wouldn't put on any suntan lotion. It gave Miss Simmons a chance to see what he was like. After lunch Papa took him on a walk to get some ice cream so I had a chance to sit and talk to her until I had said all I had to say. She listened for a long time, and then she asked some questions.

"Has Claude changed any since coming to your house?" she asked me.

"In some ways. He knows where everything is. He probably knows what's in the house as well as I do, because it's all new."

"Does he sit in the same chair for every meal?"

"Yes."

"Does he eat at regular times?"

"Mostly. He doesn't have a regular going-to-bed time."

"But he sleeps in the same bed every night?"

"He has a cot in the sewing room."

"Things like that are important for a child. For all of us. You've brought some order to his life. Are he and his mother friends?"

"She thinks so. I don't know. She talks about how free she wants him to be, but I think that's just to make her feel good about whatever she wants to do." I shut my eyes and lay down on my back on the warm sand, because all of a sudden I was feeling very sick. I had already felt a little that way in the car on the way, but the feeling had gone away. Miss Simmons asked me if I was all right, and I got up and went to a garbage can not far away and threw up. (No matter what happens, Molly Smelter always tries to be neat.) "I feel better now," I said.

As soon as Papa and Claude came back, we went to Miss Simmons's house and she put me to bed in her bed, which was even bigger than my old one. When I woke up, it was starting to get dark and everybody else had eaten dinner. I had slept for five hours. Miss Simmons brought me some tea and toast and sat on my bed. It was like being five years old again. It was great. Claude and Papa were downstairs watching television, so we could talk about what she thought we should do.

Call the police? No. Write his father? Yes, as soon as we got his address. Keep Claude? Stupid question. What else was there? Read his mother's letter to him? Yes, as soon as possible. "He may think you're hiding her somewhere," Miss Simmons said. "The idea may sound funny to you, but you don't know what's going on in that little boy's mind. Not only should he *hear* the letter, he should see it and hold it in his hands. Even if he can't read, he knows his mother's handwriting. And he should see her letter to you, too, so that he knows she told you to read his to him."

"What do you think he'll do?"

"There's no way of knowing. He might pretend he doesn't care. He might pretend he doesn't believe it. He might say that it doesn't matter where she is because she's going to be back to get him in a few days anyway. Which, of course, could be true."

"I don't think so," I said. "Mrs. Post came to Schenectady because she wanted somebody else to take him."

Miss Simmons looked at me. "Do you really think that?"

"I know it."

She got me some more toast, and then I got dressed and we went back to the lake. It was already dark, but a friend of hers who had a boat was waiting to take us out for a ride. He brought us to the middle of the lake and we watched the moon come up. It was enormous. He was Mr. Waring, and on the way home in the car, after Claude was asleep, Papa told me Miss Simmons was going to marry him in November. He touched my hand when he said it, because he knew I hated to hear it. I felt awful. "Everybody's starting new things but us," I said. "If you were younger and didn't have a daughter to take care of, you could leave Schenectady the day after the wedding and go anywhere you wanted to go."

"If I were younger and didn't have you, I'd be poorer, that's all I know."

"But still, I hold you back."

"From what?"

"From doing what you'd be doing if I wasn't here. From taking risks. I don't know."

"Molly, you and I live together and help each other. I like that. It's the most important thing in my life right now and for the next few years. I'm not looking for a change."

"But if you were on your own, without me, you'd probably leave town after the wedding and start new somewhere else."

"Probably."

"Well, that's what I mean."

"I'd rather be where I am with you at my age than anywhere else with anybody else at any age. I mean that. I don't feel as if I'm missing anything. I *like* a lot of things I don't have. I like new places. I like running a business. I like playing tennis. But I'm not foolish enough to think that I need any of those things, except possibly tennis. Do you understand that?"

"Yes."

"Good."

"But still, if I could, I'd get you to go someplace else and go with you," I said.

He didn't answer, and the rest of the way home the only thing we talked about was Mrs. Post. I told him I wanted to be the one to tell Claude what she had done, and he said all right. I don't know why I wanted that. It was as if I owed it to her. Or him. Or myself.

Chapter 14

Saturday I woke up very early, probably because I had gotten so much sleep on Friday. There were a lot of important things I had to do, including buying groceries for Aunt Aurora's wedding-eve dinner and making turkey stuffing, but there was one thing more important than anything else. I got dressed very quietly, took Mrs. Post's white dressing gown with the furry feathers down the front out of the bathroom, carried it into the back yard, dug a deep hole behind the garage, laid it carefully in the bottom of the hole, and poured the dirt back in.

That sounds like a slightly crazy thing to do, or maybe even a more than slightly crazy thing to do, but Fostra Lee Post's dressing gown really *needed* to be buried. The hole was almost two feet deep, and my arms got tired digging it, but I didn't care. When I was finished I just stood there smiling and stamping the dirt down and listening to the birds sing. It was a perfect way to start the day.

I went back inside. Uncle Shel was sitting at the kitchen table reading the paper.

"Your face is dirty," he said. "What have you been doing?"

"Digging a hole."

"It just so happens that you're the one person I want to see," he said. "I want to give you some advance information that nobody else in the world knows about, except my lawyer, of course. It's top secret. Tell me the truth, you didn't believe me yesterday, did you?"

He was always asking me questions like that, so I just looked back at him.

"About holding grudges," he said. "You didn't believe me when I said I didn't hold grudges, did you? I don't mind. You can admit it. We're in the same family now, so it's all right. You'll see how true it is pretty soon. Do you know what I'm going to do at dinner tonight?"

"No."

"Shall I tell you? Only you have to promise you won't tell anybody else. Otherwise, I can't let it out."

"Maybe I shouldn't know," I said. "Probably you shouldn't tell me."

"Cross your heart and hope to die you won't tell?"

"I don't want to know your secret, Uncle Shel."

"I'll tell you, but remember, I'm trusting you. I'm going to make your father the manager of my new shop. I'm going to give him twenty dollars a week more than G.E. offers him, whatever that turns out to be, and I'm going to take out all the old junk and put in new machinery. You want to read the contract we're going to sign? It's here in my attaché case. I just got it from my lawyer yesterday."

I wanted to walk away, but I was so mad I couldn't move. I turned my face away from him. "Uncle Shel," I said, "you are the worst man I ever met."

He acted as if he didn't hear me. He opened his attaché case and took out the contract. "It's on the second page. The first year we make a profit, I'm going to give your father twenty percent of the business, four percent a year for five years, so we'll be partners again, only the business will be bigger and more modern and better."

I made myself look at him. I felt like crying, but I wasn't

going to do it. "You could have helped him, Uncle Shel. You had money, and you got out and let him go broke. That was a terrible thing to do. And now you want him back."

"You're young, Molly, which is why you don't understand these business matters. Your papa will understand."

Aunt Aurora came down the stairs and I went over to her. "Happy Wedding Eve," I said, and kissed her. "Is Claude up?"

"He's rolling around, anyway."

I went upstairs. Papa's door was closed but I could hear him inside getting dressed. I got the letters out of my room and went into Claude's room. He was sitting on his bed wearing the red bathing suit he wouldn't wear when we were in Saratoga. I shut the door. "I want to talk to you about something important," I said, and sat on the bed facing him. "Your mother flew to California yesterday morning."

He shrugged his shoulders. "I've been to California lots."

"California's a long way away."

"No, it isn't."

"Yes, it is. It's three thousand miles."

"She's not in California."

I opened his letter and read it to him very slowly, and then I put it on the bed between us and read him the one to me. He just sat there playing with the string on his bathing suit. He didn't look angry or worried or anything.

"Claude? You heard your mother say she wanted me to read the letter to you. Do you understand what it says?"

"Sure." He stood up on the bed, and when I folded up the letter and handed it to him he kicked me in the left shoulder. It really hurt. If I hadn't grabbed him around the legs and pulled him down on my lap he would have kicked me again.

"I'm sorry your mother left, Claude, but I didn't take her away and you have no right to kick me."

"Let me go!" he yelled, and he opened the door and ran downstairs. I didn't chase him. I just sat there for a few minutes and then I went to see Papa. He wasn't in his room, so I went downstairs to the kitchen and asked Aunt Aurora where he was.

"He called Mr. Temple and left," she said. "That's all I know."

"Did you see Claude?"

"I heard him come downstairs. I think he went out the front door. There were some noises. He could be under the porch again. Right now I don't have time to worry about where everybody in the family is, Molly. I have a *few* other things on my mind."

Uncle Shel started to say something to me, but I left the kitchen and went across to the Reinauers and rang their front doorbell. I knew nobody was home, because Phillip worked at Sears on weekends and his grandparents always went to the Farmers' Market on Saturday morning, but I wanted to make sure nobody was going to disturb me.

When there was no answer after three rings I sat down and tried to think, but I couldn't. I felt completely alone and trapped, as if there was no place I could go and nothing I could do to change anything that was happening to me. The Saturday before, auction day, everything had seemed all right. We were getting rid of things, getting lighter so we could move faster. It had all looked so simple and beautiful and free, and now I was alone, with none of the things I really wanted, not even my dollhouse. I got the Reinauers' key out from under their mat and went into their house and shut the door and all the windows and started to cry. I wailed, really, walking around the downstairs of the house, until it was all out of me, and then I went back out to the porch and sat on the swing, feeling better. For a while I watched a beetle on the porch floor pulling a dead spider into its hole. There were some wide cracks in front of it, and the beetle had a hard time getting the spider across them, but it just kept working at it.

When the beetle got home I thought about the auction again, the furniture being moved out early Saturday morning, the twenty-four boxes lined up in the hall, the dollhouse, and me showing it to Mr. Potrezeski. I thought way back to being a little child at our house, with Papa and Aunt Aurora taking care of everything for me. I remembered one day when I was in the fourth or fifth grade changing all the furniture around in my room and then moving it all back the next day. I thought about all the afternoons Mary Ellen and I had spent upstairs playing with dolls and making up games. We used to send messages to each other in a basket. One of us would go downstairs to the big pantry, which had a window, and one of us would stay in my bedroom, and we'd send messages up and down in a basket tied with a rope.

I wanted to go back and be a little girl again. I even began to think about things that had happened before I was born as if I had been there, or as if they had happened to me. I saw Mama and Papa going out for walks, and their wedding. I even saw Mama as a little girl in the back yard of her beautiful house in Krakow.

I wanted to go there and be her and never come back and never grow up.

And then it was as if I had come to the end of something. There was no further back I could go, so I had to go ahead.

I stood up. I knew exactly what I should do. I got the Reinauers' key again, opened the door, and walked into the kitchen. It took me a minute to remember Mr. Potrezeski's phone number in Saratoga, and the area code, but I was sure I was going to remember it, and I did.

Mr. Potrezeski answered.

"Mr. Potrezeski," I said, "I want to sell the dollhouse."

He didn't answer for a few seconds. "Are you certain?"

"Yes."

"You find yourself in need of money?"

"Yes. That's why the price has to be high."

"How much?"

"Five hundred dollars."

"You don't have to sell it. I could give you an interest-free loan for that amount, and you could use the dollhouse as security. That way, you can have what you need without risking your property."

"No, thank you. I want to sell it. The money has to be completely mine."

"It would be yours. I wouldn't press you for it, if you're concerned about that."

"No, thank you. I know what I'm doing, and I know what I want."

"Have you told your father?"

"No, but the dollhouse is really mine. I really have to sell it. I know it's the right thing to do. I'm going to put a deposit down on the shop in Willimantic."

He was silent for a few seconds. "Perhaps we should get together and talk about it. Are you aware that a deposit is *lost money*? There's no way you can get it back once it's put down. It's really a pre-payment on the rent or the purchase price."

"I know."

"And you need the money now?"

"I want it sent to the Ziesing brothers now. I could call them and tell them it's on its way, if you'll send it."

"How about Monday? I have the morning free after ten and I could come down there. We could have lunch together."

"No, that's too late. I mean, we could have lunch then, but I need the money there today. Is there some way you could do that? Or could you get the money to somebody I know in Saratoga? It's Miss Simmons I'm thinking about. She's the one who picked me up after I came to your office. She has a cousin she could call who lives near Willimantic, and the cousin could get it out of her bank, maybe, if she has that much, and drive it to Willimantic and deliver it. No, that might not work. She's in Colorado. Also, it's Saturday."

He didn't say anything, and I realized how crazy I was sounding, so I took a deep breath and spoke slowly and quietly. "I was going to go and get a dress with my aunt this afternoon, but maybe I don't really need to do that. I could come up and see you and explain everything. I don't know the bus times, but I could find out."

"Molly," he said, "please don't misunderstand me. I'm not concerned about how the money gets transferred. I'm concerned that you do the best thing for yourself. I would feel more confident if your father knew about this. You would give up buying a new dress to come up?"

"I don't need it. I've got plenty of dresses. I'll tell Papa about it tonight, but I can't tell him until after the money is there."

Mr. Potrezeski was still silent, so again I tried to sound mature and calm and completely in control of everything. "I know five hundred dollars is a lot of money for a dollhouse, and if I had something else to sell along with it, I would. In fact, now that I think about it I do have something else. It's a pearl necklace. I don't know how much it's worth, but it might be quite a bit."

"Molly, the price is not at all the difficulty. You and I talked about the value of the house when you were here on Wednesday, and we agreed that I would pay you what you needed to get. That's all settled. Other matters are far more important. For example, your father's financial position. Can he afford to follow this up? If you put down a deposit, will he be able to raise the funds to get started?"

I wanted to lie and tell him that I knew that Papa wouldn't have any trouble, but I couldn't. "I don't know," I said. "We're coming out pretty even here, I know that. The shop is sold, so we don't owe any money, so the bank would probably lend us some."

"Where are you?" he asked. "May I call you somewhere in an hour or so?"

"Sure. I'll be home."

"Let me make a few phone calls." I wanted to tell him please not to call Papa, but he already knew how I felt about that, so I didn't say anything. "I wish you were in less of a hurry. Consultation never does any harm. Well, at least most of the time it doesn't. I'll call you in less than an hour."

I went back to the house and started to toast bread and cut celery to make turkey stuffing. (Turkey is Aunt Aurora's favorite dish.) When Aunt Aurora saw what I was doing, I had to tell her about my wedding-eve surprise dinner. "It's not a real party," I said. "It's just for you and Papa and me and Uncle Shel and Claude, but you're not allowed to do any of the work on it. You could go to Gershon's, though. They're holding the turkey there for me.

I'd go, but I'm waiting for a phone call. Maybe Uncle Shel could drive you. Make sure it's not frozen. They were going to defrost it."

"When will we go downtown for your dress?"

"As soon as the turkey's in the oven. We can go right after that." She went to get the turkey. After she left, while I was waiting for some toast to pop, I went around the house and looked under the porch. "Hiding under porches is boring," I said in a very loud voice, and a few minutes later Claude came into the kitchen and I gave him cold cereal. After he had eaten he went and got a bandage for his wrist. It was his way of making up for kicking me, probably.

Mr. Potrezeski called before Aunt Aurora got home with the turkey, and told me that a check was on its way. He had talked to Mark Ziesing and then to Alison Meyers, the Ziesings' bookkeeper, and to his own lawyer and the lawyer at the Willimantic Savings Institute.

"Thank you very much," I said. "You really saved me. Without you I don't know what I would have done."

"There is a certain amount of paperwork to be completed," he said. "Perhaps we should arrange to get together early next week."

"I'm still free Monday."

We decided he would come to the house around eleven. After I said goodbye I just stood there with the phone in my hand feeling happy, the way I feel sometimes when I've been running through the woods in the park and all of a sudden I come out from under the trees and there's nothing but open sky over me.

The rest of the day went fast. Papa came home for lunch, and right after that Aunt Aurora and I went downtown to buy my bridesmaid's dress. On the way, she began talking about Mrs. Post. "She did a terrible thing leaving her child, there's no doubt about that," she said, "but all the same she's a remarkable woman, you can't take that away from her. We met at the Camp of the Holy Family the summer before we went into ninth grade. Our session was only a week, but from the first moment, when we met on the bus on the way there, we loved each other like sisters. We had beds next to each other, and Fostra Lee would tell me stories after the lights were out. After camp was over, I wrote to her. She didn't always write back, but that's just the way she was, and when your friend does something like that, you don't get mad. It's hard for you to believe, probably, but she hasn't changed a bit. She's exactly the girl she always was."

We pulled into the Carl Company parking lot and she took out her wallet and showed me a picture. "Isn't that exactly how she looks now?" she said. "Of course, she was very mature at thirteen, much further along than any one of the rest of us, but isn't it amazing? It's as if life had never touched her at all."

"I don't think I'd want to stay thirteen forever," I said.

"That's not something a person can choose, Molly. It's a very rare woman who is as well blessed as Fostra Lee. You could learn a lot from her about how to take care of yourself. It wouldn't do you any harm. I'm going to show you something else. I was going to save them to show you Sunday, but I want you to see them now."

She took a little box out of her purse. Inside were a pair of gold, dangly earrings with tiny pearls on gold wires at the bottom. They were for pierced ears, and Aunt Aurora didn't have pierced ears, but that didn't seem to make any difference to her. "Fostra bought them in San Francisco when she was there for a Growth Channel workshop."

"They're beautiful," I said, which was true.

Aunt Aurora held one of the earrings against her ear. "I know I can't wear these right now," she said, "but maybe I'll get clips put on them, and Fostra Lee is the only girl in the world who would *think* of giving me a present like that. Not that anybody *should*, I'm not saying that. I know there are more important things. But she thinks of such things, so you mustn't say anything against her to me. I just won't hear it."

She slowly put the earrings back in the box and looked at me. "I know how you feel about her, Molly," she said. "And I know it wasn't right what she did, but Fostra Lee always has a good purpose."

I didn't say anything but I tried to look as if I understood, and we went in the store and in five minutes bought the most beautiful dress I've ever had. It was as if it was waiting there for me.

When we got home Papa had fixed all the vegetables for dinner, so I took Claude to the park to build a fire and cook marshmallows. His burn mark was all gone, and I thought it was probably time for him to find out how to build a fire right. "Go collect a bag of twigs for a fire," I said. "We'll cook marshmallows."

"I don't like marshmallows."

"Well, these are magical ones. They're different. You'll think they're really great."

"No, I won't."

An airplane flew over, and he looked up and started talking about the different airplanes he had flown on, and how many seats each one had, and how long each one was, and how much horsepower the different engines had. At first I thought he was making all the numbers up, but after a while I realized that he wasn't. He couldn't read, so he must have asked stewardesses and airline people and then just remembered what they told him, which meant he wasn't stupid. I knew that already, I guess, but it was nice to have him prove it. "Your mother's plane is probably already in California. In fact, it got there yesterday."

He didn't say anything.

"You lived in California, didn't you?"

"I never lived anywhere."

"California's a nice place to visit, anyway, I guess," I said. "Lots of people go there for vacations."

"Mama's staying there forever," he said. "She told me that a long time ago."

"When?"

"A long time ago. Different times. She's never coming back, and I'm going to stay with you forever."

I went and picked up sticks and we started a lesson on how to build a fire. The lesson didn't work because I had only five matches in the book and the wind was blowing and the wood was green. So we went to the swings and had some trips to the moon, which he still liked, and on the way home I bought him a doughnut and had one myself. He didn't learn anything, but the afternoon was hot and sitting around a fire cooking marshmallows wouldn't have been much fun anyway.

We got home around five, and Aunt Aurora had taken over the kitchen. "Don't tell me to get out," she said. "This is the last meal for you and your father that I'll cook for a while. You'll have plenty of time to cook tomorrow and the next day, you and your father both." I didn't try to talk her out of it. Instead, I went upstairs and wrote a letter to Mary Ellen. I didn't know whether I'd send it or not. It was really just a way of talking to myself.

Dear Mary Ellen,

This is my last letter until I get one from you, or at least it's my next-to-last. I'm a mother, but aside from that, everything here is pretty dull. How are things with you? The weather has been very hot. Have you been having hot weather, too?

No, I'm not pregnant. The baby is eight. (Years, not months.)

Aunt Aurora is getting married tomorrow, and I'm going to be in the wedding in a sleeveless long dress I bought at Carl's today. I don't know what kind of dress Uncle Shel is wearing. Probably lace.

I sold our dollhouse to get out of town. I will explain it when we see each other.

Did I tell you that Phillip is going out with Carolyn Bassett. Life is weird. Have you ever noticed that? I mean, I thought I was going to get free, and all of a sudden I've got to be mother to somebody else's awful kid who has a nervous habit that drives me crazy. But I never felt free the way I do right now. I feel like I can *do* things.

Weird, weird, weird. There is no P.S. on this letter because I am saving my brain for tonight.

See you,
Molly

I read the letter three or four times, put it in an envelope and addressed it and put on a stamp and walked down to the box on Union Street and mailed it. When I came home, the pre-wedding dinner was ready.

Chapter 15

T he dinner was really a Thanksgiving dinner without the pumpkin pie. We stuffed ourselves with turkey while Uncle Shel sat at the end of the table and talked and everybody else just listened. Whenever he said anything about the shop he would look at me and poke me in the side and wink. When he winked the sixth or seventh time I asked him if there was something wrong with his left eye. He just laughed and winked again.

He talked for a while about what he was going to do with the shop, and then halfway through dinner he suddenly said that he had just rented a completely furnished colonial house in Vorheesville. "We'll go there after the honeymoon, until we get a better place," he said. "You know what finally decided me? The grand piano in the living room that looks out on the garden." The house was news to everybody, including Aunt Aurora, but she acted very happy about it. The honeymoon was news to me, which is stupid because naturally everybody has one.

The best thing about dinner was that Claude carried a basket of bread to the table when I asked him to. I also got him to eat a very tiny pile of string beans by telling him that he wouldn't get any cake if he didn't. I meant it, and he knew I meant it. (I found out later that he didn't really hate beans so much.)

When dinner was over, Papa opened a bottle of champagne and made a short speech and toasted the bride and groom. Then Uncle Shel got up and made a long speech about cementing the family together and toasted Papa. As he was sitting down he took the contract out of his pocket and laid it on Papa's cake plate, getting frosting on it. "Harold," he said, "we've been through good times and hard times together, and now I'm putting in front of you the gateway to the new future. I want you to be the manager of the new business. We're going to remodel the entire shop and get all new equipment in. And as soon as we start turning a profit, you'll get four percent of the business every year for five years. We'll be partners again."

I put my fork down. "Papa and I are starting a new business in Willimantic, Connecticut," I said. "This afternoon I put a deposit on the Ziesing Printing Shop. The equipment isn't new, but Papa's seen it and says it's in pretty good shape. My investment counselor says it's a risk, but with work we should make it go."

I was looking right at Uncle Shel as I was saying this, but he didn't believe me. He grinned and poked me with his finger. "It's a joke," he said.

"No, it isn't."

"Where did you get the money?"

"I sold some property."

"It's a joke."

"No, it isn't, Uncle Shel, and please don't poke me."

His eyes opened wider and he stopped smiling. "It's a joke. You were here all day. The banks are closed."

"I did it by phone."

Papa reached across the table and touched my arm. "How much did you put down?"

"Five hundred dollars."

"What's the term?"

"If we don't buy the shop, we lose the money."

Papa shook his head. "No. What's the term? How much time do we have to raise the rest of the money?"

"We have to buy it in sixty days, or maybe we can lease it."

Papa pushed his chair back and stood up. "You and I need to have a brief business conference on the front porch." He looked at Aunt Aurora. "Excuse us, Aurora. We'll be right back."

I followed him to the porch. It was a lot cooler out there. It smelled like it sometimes does before it rains. We went to the far end and sat on the rail and didn't say anything for a long time. Then he put his arm around me. "You're a woman with a lot of class. You're dangerous, but you have class."

"Thank you, Papa." I kissed him.

"You sold the dollhouse?"

"It was the only thing I had. Mr. Potrezeski bought it."

"You have a bank account. I don't know exactly how much there is in it, but it's close to two hundred dollars."

"I didn't think of it. Besides, you would have had to sign, and you wouldn't have done it. Also, two hundred dollars wasn't enough. I called the Ziesings day before yesterday, and they told me it would have to be five hundred."

He shook his head. "Claude will have to come with us, you know. We can't leave him with Aunt Aurora. She'd be willing, but Uncle Shel would never accept him. Besides, he'd ruin him."

"If we're going to keep Claude anyway, it doesn't make any difference if we're here or there."

"No, that's not true. I talked to Doug Temple at his office this morning. Legally, as long as we're here we're just baby-sitting, but if we take Claude to another state, our position will be somewhat different. We'll be taking responsibility for him, like parents."

"O.K., that's what we'll do."

"I'm not sure you understand what taking parental responsibility means."

"Probably not, but I understand better than Fostra Lee Post does. I'm not afraid. I know it'll be work."

"It will."

"I'm really trapping you, I guess, Papa. Or at least I'm trying to."

He turned around and pulled a leaf off the lilac bush. "Poor Uncle Shel. Don't you feel sorry for him now, with nobody to run his business for him?"

"No."

"Not even a little bit?"

"Not even a little bit. I can't worry about him, Papa. I haven't got time. Anyway, he told me he didn't hold grudges. He'll be all right."

We started to walk back into the house. "Did I tell you how old the main press at Ziesings' is?" Papa asked.

"Who cares?" I said. "The new owners are very smart and they have a lot of experience in the business."

When we got back in the dining room, Uncle Shel's contract wasn't on the table any more. He said he was glad for our new opportunity, and wished us luck. "I think it's always better *not* to take charity," he said, "even when it's from a relative in the family."

Aunt Aurora was really sorry, though she didn't say so, and Claude didn't care one way or the other, as long as he was staying with us. His whole life was traveling, so one more place didn't make any difference to him.

The party went on, but with no more winks and pokes

from Uncle Shel. He left the house before we did the dishes, and we all went to bed early.

When Papa came in to say good night to me I got him to draw me a picture of exactly what our new shop looked like. It had two rooms, like the old one, but the front was long in the other direction. After he left I began to try to figure out a good name for it, but I didn't think of one until Claude woke me up around two. He was having a bad dream, and as I sat on his bed rubbing his back the name came to me, The New Place Printery.

Chapter 16

The wedding was great. Aunt Aurora wore her awful pinkish-tan dress that she had bought with Mrs. Post, but she looked beautiful anyway. Right after breakfast two bouquets were delivered to the house, a big one of white roses for Aunt Aurora and a small one of white mums for me, but before breakfast Claude and I had gone out and picked wild daisies from a field on the other side of Balltown Road and put them on the kitchen table, so they were the first flowers she saw that day, and she said she wanted us to bring them to church and put them with the other flowers on the altar, which we did.

On the way to the church Claude and I started to talk about money. His father had a lot of money, he said, and so did his mother, so he didn't need to worry about anything ever. "My mother has a million times more money than you do," he said.

"Probably. Don't grab those daisies too tight. You don't want to choke them."

"She probably has twice more than that."

"Probably."

"You don't have any money at all."

"That's not exactly true," I said, "but we don't have a lot."

"You're poor."

"Claude, when my mother was halfway between your

age and my age, she left her house, with no car or airplane ticket or anything, and walked hundreds of miles. Never for a minute in her whole life did she think she was poor, and I'm like her."

"My father's going to fly here from Mexico in his own plane and get me tomorrow."

"It's a good thing Aunt Aurora's going on a honeymoon, then, because he can sleep in her room overnight."

"Maybe he won't come exactly then."

"We'll take care of you until he does."

"Maybe he'll come and I won't want to go with him."

"Don't worry. Papa and I have class. We won't let you loose."

When we got to the church and were getting out of the car, he told Papa again how rich he was.

"Sure you are," he said. "You have Molly and me."

The greatest thing about the wedding was how many people came. Almost everybody on Palmer Avenue was there, and a lot of people from church, and Aunt Aurora felt really proud, which was right. Everybody crowded toward the front, and about half of the people went to communion after the vows were said. Papa gave the bride away, and I held her bouquet when she got the ring, and everything went exactly the way it was supposed to go. There was an enormous pile of presents in the back of the church. There were so many that Papa could hardly get into our car to drive to the Van Dyke, so Claude and I had to ride with Aunt Aurora and Uncle Shel.

The wedding luncheon was in the hotel garden, where Mr. Potrezeski and I had had breakfast, and then Claude and Papa and I drove them to the airport to get the plane for Bermuda. We watched the plane take off, and then suddenly we were all alone, the three of us, a new family.

In the car on the way home Claude leaned up against me, but when I put my arm around him he pulled away, which goes to show what happens when you expect too much too soon, or try to move too fast.

By August we were in Willimantic, Connecticut. That was a year ago. Claude is still part of the family. Since we got here he has received two letters from his mother, one inside a package with the Love Pillow in it, much better made than I thought it would be, and one with a Christmas card and a check for fifty dollars. Last March he got a postcard from his father. He had moved to Portugal. He didn't say whether he had taken the Mexican dancer with him or not.

Part of the time now I think of Claude as my son, part of the time I think of him as a much younger brother, and part of the time I think of him as a complete stranger and I wish his mother or father or somebody would come and take him away. Still, I guess I love him. At least he isn't rubbing his wrist against his pants any more, except once in a while when he's tired or frustrated. He's learning things in school and he has a friend who lives down the street. He should be in a third-grade reader and he's still only in a first, but that's better than not reading at all, and he's doing O.K. in math. The first book he took out of the library was a picture book about planes.

I can't think of anything I did last summer that I would change, except for throwing up in Saratoga.

I talk to Aunt Aurora on the phone on weekends, when the rates are down. Sometimes I remember good things from Schenectady, or I think about the dollhouse and I know that something wonderful is gone. Yesterday, out of a clear blue sky, I thought about Phillip banging down his front steps at five-thirty in the morning for his paper route, and that made me sad. Weird. But things like that don't happen much.

Willimantic is a good place to run in, if you like hills, and the school isn't bad. Mr. Potrezeski calls every once in a while, and he came here on Easter, and Mary Ellen started writing me (at last!) and she might come and visit on Christmas, or I might go down there, which would be great. And I found a good friend, Lisa Iversen, who doesn't live too far away, and if I asked for more it would be greedy, which, as I said before, I'm not. Well, not very, anyway, and never about money.